# The Day
## that Changed
### Long Island

## LUCIANO SABATINI

BQB

North Carolina

*The Day That Changed Long Island*
© 2021 Luciano Sabatini. All rights reserved.

This is a novelized version of one families' experience. Names have been changed to protect privacy.

Published in the United States by BQB Publishing
(an imprint of Boutique of Quality Books Publishing, Inc.)
www.bqbpublishing.com

Printed in the United States

ISBN 978-1-952782-29-9 (p)
ISBN 978-1-952782-30-5 (e)

Library of Congress Control Number: 2021945963

Book design by Robin Krauss, www.bookformatters.com
Cover design by Rebecca Lown, www.rebeccalowndesign.com
First editor: Caleb Guard
Second editor: Andrea Vande Vorde

# ACKNOWLEDGEMENTS

Luciano and Suzanne Sabatini would like to thank all those who helped in their recovery from Superstorm Sandy, including their children Kara, Craig and Nina; Sue's parents Nick and Shirley Canellos; her sisters and their husbands Karen & Robert McDermott and Diane & Anthony Scavazzo. Also, a special mention to all the public service workers (first responders, sanitation workers, librarians and others), the American Red Cross, and business owners of the Massapequa community who fed, sheltered and provided support to so many during this crisis.

# TABLE OF CONTENTS

# INTRODUCTION

Superstorm Sandy made landfall in the New York/New Jersey Metropolitan area on October 29, 2012. While it was gone by the next morning, the devastation it caused in less than a day made Sandy at that time the second costliest storm in our history, surpassed only by Hurricane Katrina. It created permanent physical changes, including an inlet that was carved out of the Fire Island barrier beach that still remains today. Over a thousand homes in low-lying areas were so badly damaged that they were never rebuilt. New York State bought out property owners and let nature reclaim the land.

The hurricane pummeled infrastructure of the Long Island area, destroying beach boardwalks, flooding subway tunnels with millions of gallons of saltwater, and contaminating homes with spillover from sewage treatment plants. Many small business owners didn't have the resources to rebuild and were closed permanently. Even larger facilities like the Long Beach Medical Center couldn't be repaired. Millions of tons of sand were washed ashore, clogging sewer systems and streets. In Brooklyn's Brighton Beach, the boardwalk's wooden stairs leading to the shore were completely swallowed by the sand, making the beach almost level with the boardwalk. All that remained were handrails that looked like stumps rising from the sand.

The real hardship created by Sandy can't be measured just by the destruction of material things. Many people were forever changed by Sandy as they experienced the trauma of watching their homes and communities inundated by floodwaters. Some had to live with friends and relatives for months and even years while their homes were repaired. Others had to find a new way to make a living.

This book is a novelized account of one family who lived through this terrible time.

# CHAPTER 1

# FOOLED BY TROPICAL STORM IRENE

Lucas laughed at the report on the radio. "They're making a fuss over nothing again, Sybil. When I went out to get the mail, the sky was fine."

His laugh had a certain bravado about it. Lucas was a proud, second-generation Italian-American. In his culture, it was not manly to show fear but rather to remain calm and in control.

Sybil sighed. She did not want to go through this again.

It was late August of 2011, and meteorologists were warning that a huge tropical weather system was barreling its way up the Atlantic Coast. The images on the news of huge ocean waves, power failures, flooded homes, and downed trees were intimidating but looked tame contained in a small television screen. Outside, the sky was darkening as the clouds rolled in. The wind was picking up and blowing in different directions. Leaves and other debris appeared to be racing down the street. The electric cables running from the street to the house were starting to sway like two jump ropes dancing high above the ground. According to the reporter, millions of people were preparing for the destruction that seemed inevitable. Lucas shrugged.

Sybil paced nervously behind him. "Come on, Lucas; stop procrastinating. We don't have much time to get our TVs and furniture upstairs before the storm comes."

Lucas was finishing his laundry and casually turned his head. "My dear, you're being neurotic again. We've been through this before. You're overreacting to the weather reports."

Another doomsday forecast was predicting certain disaster. They didn't need to do anything or go anywhere. They had been married twenty-eight years and lived in a split-level house on West End Avenue in Massapequa. Now sixty years old, Lucas was tall and thin with blue eyes and graying hair. He had recently retired from his career as a school administrator and had become an adjunct professor at Hofstra University. Sybil was a fifty-two-year-old high school math teacher. In contrast to Lucas, she was petite with brown hair, brown eyes, and few signs of aging. Many thought that she was much younger than her age. They had three grown children. The older two, Tara and Greg, had moved out and were living on their own while the youngest, Gina, was starting her sophomore year at a college in New Jersey.

Soon after Lucas and Sybil were married, Hurricane Gloria struck Long Island in September of 1985. Because their house was in a flood zone with canals on either side, they received warnings that they should evacuate. Some of the neighbors boarded up their homes and evacuated for higher ground. The weather folks created much hysteria, but there was relatively little damage. Gloria knocked down electric cables, some trees were blown down, and their house lost a gutter and a few roof tiles. Lucas, a lover of nature, even had fun walking outside during the eye of the storm but made a hasty retreat inside as the winds began to pick up again. Other storms had come and gone over the years with similar results: there was a lot of hype created by the media with little consequence for the homeowners.

"I'm not doing a bunch of work for nothing," shrugged Lucas, taking his time folding the laundry.

Sybil rolled her eyes frantically. She was determined to get through to him. "They're predicting over a foot of rain and massive flooding. All the furniture and electronic equipment on our ground floor will be flooded. Please show some urgency!"

Taking a deep breath, Lucas conceded. "Okay, but if this turns out to be a colossal waste of time and energy, I won't do it the next time."

After spending two hours moving furniture, computers, photocopiers, and other items into their living room upstairs, they stopped to rest. Sybil began to wonder if they should remain in their home, especially since the worst of the storm was supposed to arrive at night. She had stocked up on flashlights and candles, expecting that they would lose power, but the thought of trying to sleep through howling winds in complete darkness was unnerving to her.

The phone rang, and it was her sister Kathy. "Hi Sybil, are you still storm-proofing your house?"

"We just finished, but I'm afraid to stay here tonight."

"I have a spare bedroom. Why don't you come here?"

Sybil was relieved and accepted her offer. Now came the tough part: convincing her husband to leave with her.

"Lucas," she called to him. "Kathy has just invited us to stay there tonight. They have a bedroom for us."

He shook his head in disagreement. "If we leave the house and lose power, the water pump will shut down and the basement could flood. We just spent $25,000 finishing the basement."

"I know that we could lose the basement." Sybil had sensed the panic in his voice. "But the thought of staying here terrifies me."

"I'm not leaving," he insisted. "We've had so many false alarms over the years that I would prefer to just stay here. If we have a power failure, I can start the generator. I'm not risking that pump failing when we're not here."

Sybil sighed. "Well, I'm not staying here. I'm heading to my sister's house for the night. If you get hurt or need assistance, there will be no one to help you."

"I won't need any. I'm not about to run away from another trumped-up media event."

Her husband was stubborn and full of male ego. There was no reasoning with him.

⟨⟨━━◆◆◆━━⟩⟩

As Sybil packed up her things, Lucas noticed that most of the people on the block were leaving as well. Am I going to be the only person to remain here? he thought to himself. By late afternoon Sybil was gone, and West End Avenue felt like a ghost town. Only three families stayed behind. Lucas tried watching television to distract himself, but he was too fidgety to sit still. He paced around the house, second-guessing himself. Was he flirting with disaster by underestimating Mother Nature?

About an hour after Sybil had left, the phone rang. It was his brother-in-law Todd, Kathy's husband.

"Lucas, are you crazy? You're putting yourself in harm's way. Please leave before it's too late and come to our house."

Lucas surmised that Sybil was making one last attempt to get him to leave by having another man talk some sense into him. He replied with conviction, "Todd, I'll be fine. This storm will be a dud like all the others." His words sounded brave, but they masked the fear and trepidation he was feeling.

The house became so quiet that it was deafening. As darkness fell, he ate leftovers while listening to the pitter-patter of raindrops on the window and a growing howl from the escalating wind of the fast-approaching storm. He made sure that there was plenty of fuel in the generator and moved it closer to the house, placing it under an overhang where it would stay dry. He placed an extension cord between the water pump in the basement and the generator outside. Then he sat himself on a recliner positioned between the two. In this way, he could quickly plug them together when the power went out.

By midnight, the full force of the storm had arrived. The wind shrieked and the lights flickered. Suddenly, the television and lights went off. The water pump became silent. His house had lost power, and a quick look outside revealed that the entire block was in the dark. With a flashlight in hand, Lucas hurried outside to start the generator. With a few pulls of the throttle it started, and he connected the cords which brought the water pump back to life. He lit candles in the area surrounding the recliner. Lucas tried to sleep on the recliner, but the ferocious wind whipped the trees, and debris rained down on the side and roof of the house. After several hours, the worst of the storm had passed and daylight peeked through the clouds, but there was another danger. High tide would be peaking in two hours, and weather forecasters had predicted massive flooding in low-lying areas. Sybil called his cell phone to see how he had made out. He told her that the generator was working, and the basement was dry.

"Lucas," she said, "you should take your car and move to higher ground. You can wait out the high tide there and then go back to the house when it begins to recede."

He decided to check out the flooding in the streets for himself. As Lucas walked out his front door, he saw his next-door neighbor, Barry, a tall, thin, almost bald man in his mid-seventies. He was one of the few remaining original homeowners on the block and had bought his house on West End Avenue fifty years ago. Barry was the block historian and could tell you stories of the original homeowners who had lived there and all the challenges they faced over the years. Barry, his wife Barbara, and Lucas were among the few who hadn't evacuated their homes. The street was flooded, but the water was about even with the top of the curb.

Barry looked at Lucas with the confidence of a weather forecaster. "It looks about the same as Hurricane Gloria, and the floodwaters of that storm didn't reach our homes." Lucas agreed with him, but high tide hadn't arrived yet, so he decided to heed Sybil's advice and move to higher ground. He got into his car and slowly drove to the parking lot of a strip mall about half a mile north of his home and waited there.

At around noon, Sybil called again and told Lucas it was safe to return home. As he drove back to the house, Lucas could see that the water had reached the sidewalks but no further. When he entered his house, the generator was still working, and the basement was dry. As the neighbors began returning, they discovered their flooded basements and downed trees. Sybil returned by early afternoon and was surprised to see how much better off they were than their neighbors.

"Well, Lucas, I guess you were right," she admitted. "I might have overreacted to the weather reports."

"You weren't alone," Lucas said with a smirk. "Almost the entire block fled, and they're now paying the price."

He felt like a triumphant hero for facing the storm and saving his basement. Within two days the power was restored, the furniture was returned to its proper place, and the debris from the storm was cleaned up. It turned out to be an inconvenience but nothing more. Knowing that the $25,000 investment to finish their basement was not laid to waste by Irene was a major source of satisfaction to him.

# CHAPTER 2

# THE FRANKENSTORM

N early fourteen months later, the children on West End Avenue were preparing for Halloween. Parents were busy getting costumes for their children, visiting ghostly displays in nearby family farms, and buying pumpkins and decorations for their homes. Lucas was preparing for Sybil's birthday. He always prepared family dinners for special occasions. The children, their significant others, and grandparents were always invited to birthday dinners. He learned to cook from his deceased parents who were amazing culinary wizards in Italian cuisine. Lucas and Sybil always enjoyed having the family together for Sunday dinner, and this birthday celebration would be no different.

Listening to the weather forecast, Lucas learned that a late season monster storm was on its way. Hurricane Sandy had some unusual characteristics. It had merged with two cold fronts on its path northbound, producing a superstorm several hundred miles in diameter, much larger than Irene or Gloria. Lucas slammed his hand on the table. "Damn it, I can't believe that we're having a hurricane at the end of October," he said. "I thought hurricane season ended in September."

Sybil almost dropped her coffee. "Relax, control yourself! It's not supposed to arrive until Monday night, so it shouldn't affect our dinner."

"Okay, but I'm not moving furniture like we did for Irene. All that backbreaking work to move it, and then we had to put it back the next day."

"That's fine with me, Lucas, but there's a leak in the roof above your office. If it rains as much as they're predicting, you could have a huge puddle in your office and damage to the computer and printer."

Lucas walked down to his office to inspect the ceiling. He was looking for water stains and found a few small spots, but they were far from his desk. Nevertheless, he relented. "Fine. When Greg comes over, he'll help me put a tarp over the roof to keep it dry."

What a waste of time, Lucas thought to himself. But at least I don't have to move furniture. For the second time in a little over a year, he had to prepare for an extreme weather event. What were the odds of that? How serious could it be? By the time it reached his area, weather forecasters were predicting that Sandy would not even be a Category 1 hurricane. Its winds of ninety miles per hour would be less than Gloria and about the same as Irene, both of which were greatly exaggerated. Nevertheless, it was on every news channel, and many referred to it as Frankenstorm. For someone who had little patience, his mindset was to just go through the motions and check to see if they had all the basic necessities in case of a power outage.

On Saturday, he shopped for Sybil's dinner. She loved his spaghetti and meatballs. He would make the sauce and meatballs that evening, and the side dishes would be made Sunday morning. No way this nuisance of a storm was going to spoil Sybil's birthday celebration. Greg would help him with storm preparations on Sunday, including tying down the tarp over the roof.

On Sunday, October 28, guests began to arrive for Sybil's birthday dinner. Gina, their youngest, had arrived the day before from college to spend the weekend with her parents. Diminutive in size like her mother, with brown hair and brown eyes, Gina was a nursing student and a physically fit swimmer, an overachiever who succeeded at whatever she did. Greg looked like his maternal grandfather with dark hair and brown eyes. He had an athletic build from his many years as a long-distance runner. Like his grandfather, he had a career in business. Greg had taken the Long Island Railroad from his apartment in the city where he worked as a financial analyst. Tara, their oldest, arrived with her boyfriend, Jim. She was tall and thin like her father, with beautiful blonde hair. Like Sybil, she was a teacher, and many thought she looked like her mother. Jim was an engineer and new to the family. Dick and Sharon, Sybil's parents, were the last to arrive. A retired business executive, Dick was laughing when Lucas opened the door. "I knew I was on the right street. I could smell tomato sauce from down the block." Sharon was a homemaker and mother of three daughters. An impeccably dressed woman with a calm disposition, she was a nice counterbalance to her husband, who was boisterous by nature.

Lucas and Sybil greeted them all, and they sat in a large circle of chairs in the living room. It was time to catch up with everyone's busy lives and the news of the week. As they munched on chips and drank beer or wine, Sandy was the biggest topic of conversation.

"I hope you guys are planning to leave tomorrow before the storm," said Tara. "They're saying it is going to be a hundred-year storm."

"I don't think so, Tara," replied Sybil. "We did a lot of preparation for the last storm and evacuated, leaving your father here by himself. I don't want to do that to him again. Besides, nothing happened, and our neighbors had to deal with flooded basements when they returned. But not us, thanks to your father."

"The county executive warned that rescue workers will be giving priority to helping the elderly and disabled," said Dick. "Homeowners who stay behind will be on their own."

Gina replied, "It will be different this time. I'm not driving back to New Jersey in this storm. I'm staying here. The three of us will take care of each other."

Following along his daughter's assurance, Lucas scoffed at any hint of fear. "Dick, the media always makes it to be worse than it is because they want to increase viewership and boost their ratings. We won't be fooled again."

Sybil reminded Lucas that he had to put the tarp on the roof over his office to prevent rain from coming in. He went outside with Greg and they pulled out the tarp from the shed and tied a piece of rope to each corner. They secured the tarp to the roof by tying the ropes around the chimney, the gutter, a handrail, and a large brick. The wind was already gusting at forty miles per hour, and the tarp was flapping on the roof like a fish out of water.

"Dad, this isn't going to work," said Greg. "The tarp is way too loose, and when the real strong winds come, it'll just blow off."

Lucas sat on the roof and reflected for a moment. "You're probably right, Greg, but I'm not going to nail the tarp on the roof and create holes for water to leak through. Besides, I just want to give your mother some peace of mind that the roof is covered. This storm is just going to be another false alarm." They proceeded to put all the chairs and loose objects in the shed and gazebo before rejoining the party.

As they entered the house, Lucas enjoyed the wonderful aroma of tomato sauce that was simmering on the stove. After boiling the spaghetti al dente and mixing it with the sauce and meatballs, dinner was ready to be served. Everyone enjoyed a delicious dinner. For dessert the kids had brought Sybil's favorite—ice cream cake. All sang and wished her a happy birthday.

Soon after dinner, Sybil received a call from the principal of her school informing her that because of the coming storm, school was cancelled for both Monday and Tuesday. She celebrated the news with Lucas and the family as an extra birthday bonus.

Later they learned that all the New York City schools, as well as the entire subway system, would be closed. Despite these ominous warnings, Lucas, Sybil, and their family continued to enjoy the evening. There was no reason to fret. The storm would blow by like all the others had; it would be just another inconvenience.

❧

The next morning, Lucas suggested that he and Sybil go to the gym. There was a 9:15 spin class, and Lucas figured it would be their only chance to get out. They would have plenty of time to get back before the storm.

As they drove to the gym, Sybil noticed that Route 135 was closed due to flooding. "We'll have to take the side roads," she said.

"Well, it's the morning high tide," replied Lucas. "The flooding will recede by the time we're done with our spin class."

When they arrived at the gym, they were surprised to see a lot of activity. The spin class was almost full. This was not typical for a Monday morning.

"I guess everyone else had the same idea," said Sybil.

After a vigorous workout, they showered and met back at the car. On their drive home, they noticed a couple of stores on Merrick Road had flooded. The owners of a clothing store were loading clothes into a van. An antique shop was boarding up their windows to prevent looting. Yet, these clear red flags of what was about to come didn't seem to alarm them. Like a school fire drill, everyone goes through the motions of preparing for an evacuation, never believing that there will be a fire.

# CHAPTER 3

## SANDY IS FOR REAL

When Lucas and Sybil arrived home, they made a list of things they needed such as bottled water and a full tank of gas for their cars. Lucas decided to go to Dora's, a small, family-run grocery store, before getting gas. It was easier to find things there, and the lines would be shorter than the chain stores. At the deli counter, he overheard two women talking.

"Are you going to move your car to higher ground?" asked one of the women. "I heard that many people were going to drive their cars to the parking lot of the Long Island Railroad station."

The other replied, "I heard there are thieves stalking the parking lot waiting to break into cars when the storm arrives."

Lucas hadn't thought about moving his cars to higher ground, but after hearing the second woman, he preferred to take his chances by parking his three cars in the driveway. It was on an incline, so he could provide extra protection by moving them as close to the house as possible.

When Lucas got home, he said to Sybil, "Some people are moving their cars to higher ground, but if we do that, there is no way we can leave."

"What good would they be, anyway?" she replied. "You can't drive through flooded streets."

"I feel that we have no control if we park them far away," reasoned Lucas, "and people could steal them."

"If having them here gives you a sense of security, leave them in the driveway," suggested Sybil. "But it's a false sense of security because we aren't going to be able to escape if we have a flood."

He knew Sybil was right but didn't want to worry about thieves stealing the cars. As they waited for the storm, he felt comfort knowing that Sybil and Gina would be facing the storm with him. Lucas set up the generator so that when the lights went out, he could still power the water pump, refrigerator, and a few lamps. They were fidgety, especially Sybil who tended to get anxious easily. Lucas frequently had to calm her with his more cavalier attitude.

"I hope this passes quickly," she said.

"Don't worry," replied Lucas. "By tomorrow evening, the weathermen will be explaining why the storm just missed us."

A light rain grew steadily into an intense rainstorm. Sandy began. The gusting wind gradually increased into a gale force producing whistling sounds as it whipped through the streets. It all sounded spooky to them, but nothing to justify the doomsday reports. They had seen this script before and were bored from the inactivity.

At around 6:30 p.m., the power went out. Lucas started the generator, so some lights went back on again. Gina seemed completely unfazed by what was going on and continued to play games on her computer while her parents were monitoring the storm by radio. Flood warnings were prevalent on the weather channels, but Lucas was confident that the water pump would keep the basement dry. High tide would arrive in a couple of hours. He checked the street in front of his house at 6:45 p.m. and saw no flooding. At this point, everything that happened was expected: loss of power, backup power was being provided by the generator, and the storm was uneventful.

At 7:30 p.m., Lucas checked the street again, and this time what he saw shocked him. He called in a shrill voice for Sybil and Gina to come to the front door. As they did, all three watched in amazement at the water flooding the street, spilling over into the front lawn. The water had reached halfway up the back tire of Gina's Honda Civic and had crept up within fifteen feet of the house. As Lucas tried to process what was happening, a car drove quickly by, creating waves in the street which nearly reached the front steps. The car made it through, giving Lucas an idea.

"Sybil, our SUVs are high off the ground like the jeep that just drove by. If we left now, we might be able to escape. Gina's car will never make it, so she should go with you."

Lucas could see fear etched in Sybil's face and hear the panic in her voice. "Lucas, we talked about this earlier. You can't drive the cars in flooded streets. If we got stuck, we'd be stranded in complete darkness with no one to help us. With the rising water, we might not be able to get back to the house."

Lucas knew his wife would not consent to such a risky plan. Sybil could be very stubborn, particularly when she was anxious. As a mathematician, she always relied on thinking logically in a time of crisis, whereas Lucas reacted with his gut feeling. He was the risk-taker, and she was averse to it. While logic and probability were on her side, he knew that Gina's opinion would be important to her. Lucas felt that if they both wanted to leave, she would as well.

"I think it is worth a try," Lucas insisted. "What do you think, Gina?"

The usual carefree Gina became tense. "I'm afraid to stay in this house. Look at all the people who stayed behind during Hurricane Katrina and died. I'd rather try to get out if we can."

"I think you guys are crazy," Sybil said in a quivering voice, "but I'm not staying here by myself. Let's go."

Lucas got into his car and backed out of the driveway first, then Sybil and Gina followed in Sybil's car. They proceeded down the flooded street several feet apart. Lucas knew that he had to go slowly since he didn't want the water, which was a foot deep, to flood the electrical system. As he proceeded to the corner, he could see that the water at the intersection traveled eastward rapidly. Lucas surmised that the storm surge had breached the bulkhead of a nearby canal and was flooding the streets. He texted Sybil to let her know that he was going to try to cross the intersection, but not to follow him until he made it to the other side.

As Lucas drove halfway through, the strong current pushed against the driver's side of the car, while murky water oozed in through the bottom of the door. As the car cleared the intersection, it suddenly stalled out. Realizing that his escape plan wasn't going to work, he texted Sybil to return to the house. He needed to move the car closer to the curb rather than leave it in the middle of the street.

Lucas made several attempts to start the car when suddenly he heard a loud siren coming from the engine. Since the car didn't have an alarm system, he was baffled as to what caused the siren. He began to shiver, thinking that the siren was signaling danger. Perhaps the car was going to burst into flames. As he exited the car and stood in the water, he heard two other cars down the block with similar sirens. He realized the meaning of the siren. It indicated that the car's engine was being by infiltrated by water and was about to expire. In the midst of wind, darkness, and flooding, it was eerie to hear the wails of dying cars penetrating the night.

In less than a minute the sirens stopped. All Lucas heard was the wind thrashing tree branches and he could see the smaller trees bending to the force of nature. He shuddered at the unnerving sound of water moving through the streets and inching closer to the homes. He never felt so isolated and alone. How stupid he was to take such a risk! Sybil's warning about becoming stranded with no one to help if they failed to escape came to fruition. Fear gripped his body, and he started to tremble. It was difficult for him to think, but he had to restrain his feelings to remain in control.

He was only about 250 feet away from his house, but that short distance was fraught with danger. He could see natural and man-made debris—children's toys, lawn signs, shoes, balls, branches, leaves, pinecones—floating on the surface of the water, but he couldn't see the bottom. What if he stepped into a hole or tripped on something and fell? If he twisted an ankle or broke a bone, he might not be able to get back. Even more frightening were all the damaged electrical wires.

In Massapequa, the electric cables were all above ground on telephone poles. During extreme weather events, there were frequent blackouts because falling trees or branches had snapped cables. Lucas feared electrocution if a live wire was snapped and landed in the water. He momentarily thought about staying in the car. If he did, the rubber tires would offer protection against electrocution. But then he remembered the images of victims of Katrina who waited on the roofs of their cars and homes expecting to be rescued. Many never were. Besides, he didn't know exactly when high tide would reach its peak. At the speed the water was rising, there could be two additional feet or more in a short time. After weighing his options, he made the decision to try to get back to his house.

The water level had reached a few inches below his knee. Barring any mishaps, he should be able to make it back to his house in several minutes. The most difficult part of the way back was crossing the intersection where the water moved most rapidly. As he began to cross, he could see and even feel debris in the water floating by. A dark, furry object brushed against his leg which caused him to jump. As it flipped over, he could see a tail. Some unfortunate animal was being carried by the storm surge.

After he crossed the intersection, the water moved more slowly, and he was able to avoid harmful debris. Lucas tried to walk on sidewalks or walkways where the flooding was shallower but two fallen oaks forced him back into the middle of the street. After about twelve harrowing minutes, he finally made it back to his house. Lucas was happy to see that Sybil's car was in the driveway. Gina's Honda Civic had floated to the street. His wife and daughter greeted him as he opened the door.

Sybil threw her arms around him in a fierce embrace. "Thank God, you made it back."

"We almost went back out to look for you," added Gina.

They held each other for a few moments and were happy to be together again, but this nightmarish evening was far from over.

# CHAPTER 4

# THE FIGHT AGAINST MOTHER NATURE

Lucas looked into the garage. Water was already seeping in through the bottom of the door. Because the oil burner was in back of the garage, the door leading into the house was fireproof and heavy. Lucas felt that the garage and fireproof doors would create a formidable barrier to the floodwaters. The only other place that water could enter was a back door leading to the yard. The generator was outside this entrance and for the door to be completely closed, it had to be unplugged. Disconnecting it meant they were in the dark again, but they had plenty of flashlights and candles.

The house had a split-level design; the basement had a TV room with a couch and chairs. The ground floor, which was comprised of the family room with a bathroom, bar, and Lucas's study, was the most vulnerable to flooding. The kitchen, dining, and living rooms were seven stairs above the ground floor, and another short flight of stairs led to the bedrooms and two more bathrooms. Gathering in the family room, Lucas, Sybil, and Gina made a battle plan to defend their home.

"There are only two places where water can enter," began Lucas. "The garage and backyard door. If we seal the spaces between the doors and their frames, that should minimize the amount of water getting in."

Sybil dashed for the linen closet. "Let's get as many rags as we can and start stuffing the spaces around the doors."

They gathered linens—bath towels and kitchen rags—and filled in the crevices.

"Some water is still going to leak through," said Gina. "Perhaps we should get some pots and buckets to catch the water and empty them in the sink."

"Great idea, Gina," agreed Lucas. He felt proud of his daughter's ingenuity. "Let's get these items from the kitchen and place them near us."

The plan was to keep the water out of the basement and ground floor as much as possible. The family hadn't planned for the damage that was about to take place. Unlike with tropical storm Irene, they hadn't moved furniture and electronic equipment from the ground floor to the living room, so all these things were exposed to flooding.

"Is this really happening?" asked Gina. "I feel like we're in the movie Titanic waiting to go down with the ship."

Lucas could tell she needed reassuring. He wanted to say something, but his wife jumped in.

"No matter what happens to the house, all that matters is that we aren't hurt."

The three of them held hands tightly and waited for the water to enter.

The wind howled against the house. The garage door rattled as if announcing that the enemy was nearby. Water began to seep through the fireproof door. They tried to stuff more towels in the crevices, but as the water pressure increased, the towels came out. It became a losing battle. Using the pots and buckets now became a better strategy. At first it was easy to catch the water since there was a small step beneath the door. Buckets were filled and emptied in the bar sink twelve feet away. As the storm surge increased and the water level rose, it pushed against the door, and more water emerged from the side and the bottom.

"We need to be more efficient," said Lucas. "We are wasting

too much time and energy going back and forth to the sink. Let's do what the old firefighters used to do before they had fire trucks; form a line where we can pass the buckets down to each other and to the sink."

That seemed to help for a while, but as the buckets and pots were filling up more quickly, the pace of passing them down was becoming more and more frantic.

Sybil said, "I feel like I'm in that episode of I Love Lucy where Lucy and Ethel couldn't keep up with the chocolates on the conveyer belt, so they started eating them, but there is no way that I am downing this water."

They laughed nervously, easing their tension a bit.

After roughly forty-five minutes of this losing battle with Mother Nature, the sink was no longer draining, and the water was now backing up and spilling out on to the floor. They couldn't stop the inevitable. Water now flooded the entire ground floor and was filling up the basement. As it flowed down the four steps leading to the basement, it sounded like a waterfall; a sickening sound that made them feel helpless. They retreated upstairs.

"Let's salvage what we can," said Gina. "I'll get the television from the basement." Sybil followed her downstairs and grabbed her wedding album and laptop computer. Lucas took his briefcase and the books he used to teach his course at Hofstra University.

"Dad, what about the fish in your aquarium?" Gina pleaded. "I know how much you enjoy them."

"It's too late, Gina," replied Lucas. "My office is a mess, and I have no place to put them. Thanks to your quick thinking, we saved some important items."

Exhausted, they sat for several minutes in the living room, which thankfully was dry.

Lucas assessed their situation. The radio and cell phones got wet while they fought the floodwaters and were no longer working. It was 8:50 p.m., and he wondered if high tide had peaked. He opened the sliding glass door to the deck to see how high the water had reached in the backyard. It was almost even with the deck, which was four feet above the ground. He then looked at the flight of stairs leading down to the ground floor. Water that was rushing in had now slowed. Only two steps separated the water from the living room level. At the front of the house, the storm surge had submerged five of the seven steps leading to the front door. The house was like an island in the sea. Only about a foot to eighteen inches separated the flood from the living room level. Their neighbors across the street, Rick and Kelly, stood outside their front door. Lucas shouted, "Are you guys okay?"

Kelly responded, "Yes, but we're trying to figure out an escape route. We have a blow-up raft but aren't sure both of us and the dogs can all fit."

Lucas replied, "Be careful, there's a lot of debris in the water that can puncture your raft. If you decide to go, I'll come over and hold the raft so you can get in."

"Okay, thanks Lucas," said Rick. "I'll signal you with my flashlight if we decide to leave."

"Do you know when high tide is supposed to peak?"

Rick shouted, "about 10 p.m."

Lucas informed Sybil and Gina that the water would be rising for at least another hour. It took only two hours for the floodwaters to reach a depth of three feet. The living room would almost certainly be flooded before reaching high tide. They needed an emergency plan.

Gina had an idea. "Greg's bedroom lies right above the roof of your study, Dad. If we opened the window, we could crawl out onto the roof and wait there for help."

Lucas liked the idea. They could wait for the tide to change on the roof and then escape to higher ground during low tide. But there was one obstacle—Lucas had never removed the air conditioner from the window after the summer. His tools were in the garage, and there was no way he was going to be able to get them. Using knives and other kitchen utensils, he tried to loosen the screws that kept the air conditioner in place. After several minutes, he managed to remove them. As he lifted the air conditioner, a strong gust of air came through the window, knocking Lucas off balance. He tried to break his fall with an arm and landed hard on his back. He was more stunned than hurt, but he found himself shivering and crying. The accumulation of fear, frustration, and tension of the last few hours caught up to him. He was supposed to be the protector of his family, but he was failing them miserably.

Sybil grabbed his arm and kicked the air conditioner away from him.

"Lucas, why are you upset? Are you hurt?" she asked.

Gina rushed into the room. "Did the air conditioner fall on you, Dad?"

Lucas shuddered and shook his head. "No, I'm all right. Just frustrated that nothing is going our way. I just need a minute to regroup."

"The wind is too strong out there," Sybil warned. "If we go on to the roof, we may get blown off."

"Mom, if we sit on the roof and push our backs against the house with our legs, we'll anchor ourselves," said Gina. "Then locking our arms together will give us more stability."

"Is it enough to protect ourselves?" replied Sybil. "We've taken some risks tonight that haven't gone our way. You and Dad are too willing to take chances."

"We can also position ourselves behind the chimney, which will give us some protection from the wind," added Lucas. "This is just an emergency plan, and we hopefully won't have to go out there."

"Okay," conceded Sybil. "I don't have a good feeling about this, but I'll do whatever you guys think is best."

"Why don't the two of you get some warm clothing in case we have to go onto the roof," advised Lucas.

Sybil and Gina rummaged through their closets and found rain gear and sweaters. They waited for the next move but were exhausted and lay down to rest. Lucas stood guard and waited for the flood to invade the living room. He never received a signal from Rick and Kelly. They must have changed their minds, he thought to himself. It was good news. They would have gotten stranded in the middle of the storm like he did.

Suddenly, there was a loud crash. His first thought was that the fireproof door had given way and a large wave of water was about to ascend the steps flooding the living room. But when he opened the door and looked down the stairs, it was eerily quiet. The sound of the waterfall had now ceased since the basement was flooded almost to the ceiling. With his flashlight in hand, Lucas walked down a few steps into the water. Both doors were still closed and intact. He then noticed a large gash on the wall behind the bar, and the refrigerator was on the floor. Apparently, the water had lifted the refrigerator until it crashed into the wall and then fell on its side. He was at least relieved that nobody had gotten hurt, and a tsunami had not engulfed his living room.

Lucas remained vigilant throughout the night. At about 10 p.m., the water level was less than a foot from the living room, but it never got higher. He kept checking periodically. At about midnight his last observation revealed the water level had dropped significantly. The onslaught had finally ended. He went to tell Sybil and Gina the good news and found them sound asleep. Not wanting to wake them, he lay down and fell asleep as well. He was relieved that they were all safe. Perhaps he had not failed after all.

# CHAPTER 5

# THE MORNING AFTER

"Lucas, wake up," said Sybil. "The storm's over."

It was about eight a.m., and the street was dry. Lucas walked down the stairs to the ground floor. There were streaks of water, but it was basically dry. But the basement, because it was below ground, still had about three feet of water, and the furniture floated on the surface like cubes of ice in a drink. The garage was nearly dry, but the base of the garage door had been pushed in at least a foot. That explained why it was not an effective barrier in keeping the water out. The force of the water had created a tunnel under the door, allowing the water in.

The backyard was like a war zone. An entire row of fifteen-foot-tall pine trees that had formed a boundary between his property and his neighbors were mangled and twisted. Some were uprooted and lying on the ground. Behind the backyard gate a tremendous amount of debris had piled up. Tomatoes and peppers from the vegetable garden, pinecones, wood chips, tree branches, and empty pots formed a pile about three feet high. Lucas surmised that, as the water retreated with the changing of the tides, all this debris floating in the water could not fit through the bottom of the door and was filtered out. He would have to call his gardener to see what could be done about the mess.

As he walked to the front of the house, the Honda Civic and Sybil's SUV had been flooded and ruined by the water. He couldn't start any of the cars. Lucas's SUV, which had died during the storm, was on the next block. He could not find an available tow truck driver to move it to the front of his house for two days because every AAA service station was overwhelmed with people needing help. Other cars strewn up and down the street were abandoned, lifeless hulks. Some of his neighbors were outside inspecting the damage to their properties. Barry, the elderly neighbor who had remained in his house during tropical storm Irene, was particularly upset. His head hung low, and he was almost inaudible. He, too, had lost his cars, and his house had extensive damage.

"When I paid off my mortgage ten years ago, I dropped my flood insurance," said Barry. "I'm not going to be able to pay for all these repairs on my own."

Another neighbor chimed in: "I have flood insurance, but I doubt it will pay for all this damage."

As dire as things appeared to these homeowners, it could have been much worse. Many tens of thousands of Long Islanders caught a break because Sandy wasn't classified as a hurricane when it made landfall near Brigantine, New Jersey. If it had, only those with a hurricane insurance rider in their homeowner's policy would have been able to file a claim. Lucas was fortunate because the bank that held his mortgage required flood insurance, which he had through FEMA. However, he never read the policy and didn't know what damage would be covered.

Lucas and his neighbors began cleaning some of the debris that littered the street and front lawns. They pushed small trees and big branches off the street so vehicles could pass by. Ironically, with all the destruction surrounding them, it was a beautiful day with temperatures in the mid-sixties. The sun was shining, and the sky was a deep blue color. It was so calm and serene that it felt unreal, like a bad dream. One neighbor remarked, "It's hard to believe that just twelve hours ago, the world appeared to be ending."

"It does feel surreal," replied Barry, "How can there be such extremes in just a matter of hours?"

"Perhaps it's Mother Nature's way of laughing at us for underestimating her," said Lucas.

As Lucas went back in to inspect the remainder of his home, he discovered that he had no hot water because the storm surge had flooded the oil burner. The washer and dryer in the basement were ruined, and none of the kitchen appliances were working. Few homes escaped damage. He heard from a neighbor that 90 percent of homes on Long Island had lost power. Schools, government offices, public transportation, and most businesses were closed for the remainder of the week. It was difficult to get any information about what was going on. Many cell phone towers were damaged so mobile phone calls often didn't get through. Unless one had a battery-operated radio, it was hard to access news channels. Some neighbors reported that the Red Cross was setting up emergency stations in local parks to offer food and assistance. All hotel rooms had been booked prior to the storm by those living near the water, so there were no hotel vacancies in the area for people whose homes were now uninhabitable. Friends and family members took in many of these people while others were left homeless.

Lucas discovered that the landline phone in his office was working. Sybil called Greg, Tara, and her sisters and parents to make sure that everyone was okay. All were fine, and none had experienced the extensive flooding to their homes or apartments. Sybil was great at damage control when it came to home repairs. She watched all the home improvement shows on television and immediately started reaching out to friends and acquaintances to see who could help them. With an outgoing personality and great social skills, Sybil knew so many people from work and the community.

"Lucas, I just spoke to my friend Cheryl, and she told me that her husband has a restoration business. If we can get the water out of the basement, he can rip out all the sheetrock from the damaged walls and set up fans to dry the damaged rooms. This has to be done quickly because once mold starts to form, we'll have to leave the house."

"Okay, that sounds like a good plan. The best way to drain the water is to get the pump working."

He needed power to start the pump, so he went outside to check on the generator. Lucas pulled the throttle several times, but nothing happened.

"Sybil, the generator is not working. Let's call the water pump company. Perhaps they can drain the water with one of their trucks."

Sybil was able to reach the company that installed and maintained the water pump. They would send a crew later in the day to drain the water from the basement. Meanwhile, furniture had to be removed from three rooms so that workers could do their job. The waterlogged furniture was way too heavy for Lucas, Sybil, and Gina to move. Fortunately, Gina was a socialite like her mother and had many friends. She offered to get some of her friends to help with the heavy stuff.

The loud sound of sanitation trucks passed up and down the streets. People brought damaged things to the curb where sanitation workers loaded up their trucks and carted them away. Within an hour, Gina's boyfriend and his cousin arrived and moved the heavier furniture to the curb. Other friends came later to help them as well. By early afternoon, lined along the curb in front of their home was a pile of furniture, books, electronic equipment, exercise machines, a refrigerator, wet garments, and bathroom paraphernalia that stretched for thirty feet. Gina, who'd always had great timing for comic relief, took a picture of Lucas working out curbside on his beloved elliptical machine for the last time. She posted it to her Facebook page with the caption, "There are some things that we just can't let go of. Dad working off the stress of Sandy." Lucas laughed, reminded by his daughter that humor was their best ally.

The water pump company finally arrived, and with a huge vacuum hose in their truck proceeded to drain all the water from the basement and out to the curb. Sybil was amazed to see so much foam. "guess I had a lot of laundry detergent in the basement," she remarked to the worker. "It must have dissolved in the water to produce all this foam."

He smiled at her. "Lady, the foam is not soap. Seawater produces this kind of foam when it's drained from a home. This is a different of kind of water; not rainwater from the sky or groundwater from below the surface, but saltwater that came from the bay."

Marine life lived in this water. Some of Sybil's neighbors reported finding dead fish and other marine animals in their flooded homes.

The storage restoration company finally arrived and drew lines on the walls indicating where the water damage had reached. They cut and removed all sheet rock that stood six inches above the lines. "Are we going to be able to sleep here tonight?" Lucas asked one of the workers.

The man nodded. "There will be a lot of dust, so close all the doors leading to the upper floors. That will prevent the particles from going upstairs, and you should be okay to stay."

After they were finished, all that remained of the lower floors of the house was a skeleton of its former self. The only thing left of the walls were the wood studs. The family room, bar, garage, and study were completely open, lending an unobstructed view of those rooms from any point on the ground floor. The wooden beams were soaked, so the workers set up floor fans to dry them. The spinning blades were so loud that it was hard to hear when someone spoke. The workers also covered the bare wall between the ground floor and garage with plastic to cut down on the draft and cold air from the garage. The workers told them that they would have to replace all the electrical outlets that were below the waterline of the flood before restoring power to the house. The salt would corrode the affected outlets and electrical wiring.

When the men finally left in the early evening, the house became dark, cold, and spooky. Their voices echoed in the rooms that were stripped of their walls. Lucas, Sybil, and Gina had canned tuna fish for dinner; all refrigerated foods were spoiled by now. There was no television to watch or computers to entertain them. A few candles provided some light for reading or playing word games. As unnerving as it was to stay in a hollow house, at least no one was injured, and the worst was over. While they were still feeling the trauma from the storm, they were grateful that they still had a home to stay in. Thousands of Long Islanders did not have this luxury. While they took the first important steps to fix the house that day after the storm, they realized they had a long journey ahead of them before normalcy could return to their lives.

# CHAPTER 6

# LIFE IN A POST-SANDY WORLD

The second day after the storm was Halloween, one of Sybil's favorite holidays. As they sat eating a cold breakfast, she said, "I love giving out candy to the children on the block and seeing how they're dressed. I wonder if it will be cancelled." Before the storm, Sybil had prepared little packages for the children on the block as she did every year. How disappointed she would be if no one came trick-or-treating.

"I don't see how they can have it," replied Lucas. "Doorbells probably aren't working, and people are focused on getting through this crisis. Besides, parents aren't going to let their children go up and down the block when there is still so much debris on people's lawns and walkways. It's not safe. Kids are just going to have to understand that things will not be the same for a while."

A dejected Sybil replied, "We are just going to have to make it up to them when things are back to normal."

The New York Marathon was supposed to take place Sunday, November 4. Nearly thirty thousand people had registered and paid the $300 entrance fee to be in the event. One of Sybil's friends, Maggie, was registered for it. She had been training for months.

Sybil asked her, "Do you still want to run in it?"

"I do," said Maggie. "Since I have been training for so long and I was lucky to finally get a chance to be in it, but I know that the police would have to be taken away from the emergency work they are doing for the city."

There was much discussion in the media about letting the

race take place as a show of resiliency and a distraction from the terrible stress people were feeling. Others felt that going forward with the marathon would show insensitivity to the suffering of tens of thousands who needed help from city workers. Ultimately, the later view prevailed, and the New York City Marathon of 2012 was cancelled. Maggie felt that it was the right thing to do. As she told Sybil, she felt it would have been selfish of her to participate in the race at the expense of so many who were hurting. However, she was angry that the city didn't refund the participants. No one was refunded the $300 participation fee; they weren't even given a credit towards the next year's race.

"What a disappointment," said Sybil. "This is the first time that the marathon has been cancelled. I feel bad for all of you who have trained for so long but putting people first during such a crisis makes sense to me."

⊰◈⊱

Each autumn, Lucas served as a volunteer for an annual fundraiser sponsored by the American Foundation for Suicide Prevention. It was a walk held at Old Westbury Gardens in early November, and the event raised hundreds of thousands of dollars for research in suicide prevention. Because there was no power at the venue and large trees had fallen on parts of the walk path, the management at Old Westbury Gardens decided to cancel the event. Lucas felt the heartbreak of every organizer who had spent months in preparation, only to lose the opportunity to raise money at the event.

There were many other activities in the coming weeks that were cancelled. Professional sports games, school events, family parties, weddings, conferences, and business events were postponed or never took place. The financial cost, and perhaps more importantly the emotional price, was enormous. Things that brought happiness and purpose to people's lives were taken away. Instead, the community now had to devote their time and resources to repairing their homes.

Lucas turned his attention to filing insurance claims.

"There are so many forms to file, Sybil: GEICO for our lost cars, FEMA for flood insurance, homeowner's insurance for wind damage, and other things that we are not even aware of yet. I can't fax anything, and the postal service is delayed because of all the storm damage."

"Try to be patient, Lucas," advised Sybil, who sensed how annoyed he was. "Everyone is in the same boat, so I'm sure the companies will make allowances. Just do one at a time, and then we'll figure out the best way to submit them."

As they slogged through all the forms, Lucas soon discovered that these polices were not comprehensive. None covered the extensive damage done by the saltwater to his property. It killed many of the plants and small trees in the backyard and all the shrubs in front of his house. With no content insurance, they would have to pay to replace all the furniture. Lucas's office phone was a landline, and one of the few telephone lines on the block that was working, so it was easier for him to contact the insurance companies. Once his neighbors found out, they asked if they could use his phone. Soon his office became a call center visited by his neighbors who were filing insurance claims or trying to reach restoration companies.

With the mail service delayed, people had to rely on fax machines to submit their paperwork, but few had a working fax line. The public libraries became a lifeline for many. When the Massapequa library regained power, they opened their doors to the public for extended hours. They not only provided use of their fax machine, but they also served coffee, tea, and refreshments to storm victims, and a place to stay during the day as the weather got colder. The local government really extended themselves during this time of crisis. In addition to the libraries, sanitation workers, police, volunteer firefighters and parks department employees were there to help the community. Local businesses tried to help their patrons, and many eateries cooked food for those who had nothing to eat. They collaborated with the American Red Cross workers to assure that people were getting the assistance they needed. Lucas was able to fax his claim to FEMA but knew he was one of many thousands. He would have to wait a while before hearing from them.

———◆———

Despite the extensive work on the house, Sybil realized that their most immediate need was getting a car. Gina had to get back to her college in New Jersey, which had lost power during the storm but was now reopening. Lucas tried renting one from the local car rental companies.

"Sybil, I'm so frustrated. I've called Avis, Hertz, and Enterprise. None of them have a car left. We are stuck without transportation."

"I think we are going to have to try to borrow a car until the insurance company processes our claim and reimburses us for our lost vehicles."

Lucas frowned. "No one is going to give us a car when there is such a shortage."

"Since my parents are retired, they can probably do without a car for a few days. I will ask my father."

Sharon and Dick, who were living in an apartment building in Garden City, didn't suffer any damage from the storm. Their building never lost power. They wanted to help and so agreed to lend their car to Sybil for a few days. This way she could drive Gina back to school.

Later that day, Dick drove to Massapequa and was shocked to see abandoned homes, some crushed by tree branches. There was much activity; people were moving flooded furniture out of their homes and picking up piles of debris from their properties. Some looked distraught while others seemed stunned and expressionless. It saddened him to see people living in trailers next to their homes. One family was even living in their boat that was parked in the driveway.

When he arrived at their house, Sybil directed him where to park.

"Thank God you guys are okay," said Dick as he hugged them both. "I saw pictures on the news of the damage on the South Shore, but seeing block after block of people's belonging on the curb and living in trailers made me realize how devastating the storm was. I'm glad you're taking stock of the situation to see what needs to be done."

"Thanks for coming, Dad," said Sybil. "We're just trying to prioritize and see what needs to be done first."

"Is there anything else I can do?" offered Dick.

She took the car keys. "No, this car will be a lifeline, so you have already done a lot. I'll drive you home and have the car back to you in a few days."

"Okay dear," said Dick as he got in the car. He squeezed her hand. "Just take it one day at a time so you don't get overwhelmed. It will take a while, but you will get over this."

Sybil smiled at him with tears in her eyes as they drove off.

⟶◈⟵

Lucas wanted to restore power to his house. Most of his neighbors had generators which enabled them to keep the stove, refrigerator, and some lights on. His generator was flooded during Sandy, but now—two days later—perhaps it had dried. Lucas went to the backyard and pulled the throttle of the generator several times. Nothing happened. His next-door neighbor Sam, a young man with a wife and two young children, was watching.

"Lucas, you won't get that started. The saltwater has probably already damaged the wiring."

"Is yours working, Sam?"

"Yes, but I use it sparingly. I'm very low on gas. We've been staying with my wife's parents. I don't want the kids around this mess. I've been coming when necessary to meet people who have offered to help and have been doing some cleanup."

Lucas had known Sam for about two years. They had moved in recently, and he was always friendly. He and his wife were both medical professionals and nice people who always extended themselves to neighbors in need. Lucas thought that perhaps the two could work an arrangement that would benefit both.

"Since you're not here very often," said Lucas, "is it possible that I can use your generator when you are away? I would buy gasoline and be responsible for making sure the generator is working properly."

"Sounds good to me," said Sam. "Could you also keep an eye on my house and let me know if something happens?"

"Sure, I'll keep you informed." Lucas was very appreciative of his neighbor's willingness to share the generator. His relationship with Sam had taken a big step forward. Before all this, their friendship entailed occasional small talk, but this crisis had made them partners.

To make this plan work, he needed to get large containers for gas. He had only two-gallon containers. That would keep the generator going for a few hours. He needed five-gallon containers. Sam had one but he needed more. As with everything else, the stores were out of them, so Sam had to ask his neighbors if he could borrow a couple.

"Sorry, but we need them for ourselves," was the most common reply he received.

Finally, he saw someone selling house and auto supplies from the back of his truck on Sunrise Highway.

"Hi, do you happen to have five-gallon gas containers?" inquired Lucas.

"Yes, I do," said the friendly man who looked quite happy considering it was such a stressful time. "I have two left."

"I'd like to buy them both," replied Lucas.

"Okay, that will be $200," said the vendor.

Lucas raised his eyebrows and answered sarcastically, "Are you including the gas at that price?"

"No, just the containers," he responded. "Everyone is out of them, and I could probably get more for them if I wanted to."

Lucas hated to be ripped off, especially by a smiling individual who had self-interest in his heart rather than compassion for others. However, he needed the cans and paid him the money. While Sandy brought out the best in many people as family, neighbors, friends went out of their way to help one another, it also brought out the greed in people, like the unscrupulous stranger. Why would people seek to profit in such circumstances? Lucas thought to himself. Do they feel empowered by knowing that they have things that others need? Wouldn't kindness produce a better self-esteem than a few extra dollars in one's pocket? With cans in hand, he walked away, demoralized by the experience.

# CHAPTER 7

# THE GASOLINE CRISIS

Lucas planned on driving Dick's car to the nearest gas station, filling the cans up, and getting Sam's generator going. Sybil also came to help. The couple went to several gas stations, and they were all closed. Lucas finally pulled up to Bart's Mobile Station. They knew him well since they had their cars serviced there. Lucas thought he'd ask him what was going on.

"Hi Bart. Why are you closed? We haven't seen any gas stations open in the area."

"Lucas, electricity is needed to pump gas. We lost power like everyone else."

"Do you know anyone around who is open?" asked Lucas.

"There is a Getty station on Broadway, about two miles north of here," replied Bart. "Be prepared to wait on a long line. Most stations that have power are rationing gas and are open only for a few hours."

"We're just trying to fill containers for our neighbor's generator," explained Lucas. "Do you think we will have a problem?"

"Yes, because thousands of people are doing the same thing. To make it worse, people are hoarding; they're refilling their fuel tanks before they need to. You may want to drive by to see when they are pumping gas and how much you can purchase."

Lucas heeded Bart's advice and drove by the Getty station on Broadway. There was a line of cars that stretched over two blocks. A huge sign above the pumps read "7 Gallons Per Customer," but he didn't see anyone with containers. Lucas asked a young male attendant, "I need to fill gas containers for my generator. Can I do that here?"

The young man answered, "You're going to have to come back later. We do cars from nine to noon, and customers with containers from two to five in the afternoon. We sell gas until we run out, so you may want to come early."

Lucas and Sybil left and came back at 1:30 p.m., thinking that they would be at the front of the line. They were quite surprised to see that a queue had already formed of about forty people, all standing there with multiple containers.

"Sybil, do you think it's worth waiting? Maybe we should try someplace else?"

"I think any gas station around here will have a long line."

"What if we drove to the North Shore?" suggested Lucas. "They seemed to have sustained less damage. There may be more stations opened with shorter lines."

"We don't know that to be true, Lucas; 90 percent of Long Island lost power. We would also be wasting fuel driving there not knowing what we would find. These are very trying times that require patience, which is not your strong suit. There is no quick fix here, and I am willing to wait on the long line."

Lucas relented and agreed to stay. They parked the car and joined a weary-looking group of people. By two p.m., there were over a hundred people forming a line that stretched two blocks. It was a slow and arduous process as each person filled their containers with seven gallons. It looked to Lucas that everyone on the line was probably thinking the same thing: I hope the gas doesn't run out before I get there. Given the level of stress that people had been living under, customers were patient and respectful to one another until a car pulled up on the other side of the pumps that people were using. Out of the car came a very confident-looking young man wearing a suit and tie. He had a certain swagger, like he was someone of importance.

The driver went to the attendant and said something. He then proceeded to start pumping gas into his car. One angry man shouted, "What are you doing? These hours are reserved for customers with containers."

The young man replied, "I am a business associate of the owner, and he has given me permission to fill up my car."

Another angry customer responded, "That's not what the sign says. You're taking gas from people who have been waiting here for nearly an hour."

"The owner and I are partners, and I need the fuel for my business."

A third customer joined in, "The sign doesn't say there are exceptions. Besides, you could just be making up a story to cut the line."

The angry exchange of words was getting people riled up. Some were shouting at the business partner. "Go away! Come back when cars are scheduled to be here." The wind was picking up, and they were feeling cold and fed up with this encroacher.

"Stop pumping gas and get out of here," demanded another customer. People left the line and began approaching the young man, forming a small mob.

Sybil clung to her husband. "Lucas, this is getting scary. Maybe we should leave before a fight breaks out."

"No way I'm leaving," Lucas said defiantly. "To walk away after waiting this long is ridiculous. This jerk who's trying to cut the line should be the one leaving."

Three men walked up to the business partner. He looked very nervous and stopped putting gas into his car. He protested, "I have permission from the owner. We are business associates, and you have no right to threaten me."

"We don't know who you are," replied a burly middle-aged man in a deep voice. "We need fuel to keep our families warm, to keep our generators running, and for our cars. We are talking about survival, mister. I don't care about your business needs. Unless you get the owner to come down and explain to us why your needs are more important than ours, you should leave."

The business associate went to the young attendant who was inside the office. It looked like he was trying to get him to intervene. The attendant didn't want to get involved and stayed inside. The stubborn young man decided on one more approach to quell the angry customers. "I will call the owner and let him explain to you that I have permission to get gas."

The burly man replied, "That's not good enough. How do we know that the person on the phone is the owner? He must come here and explain to all of us why you should get special treatment."

The young man tried calling the owner from his cell phone. When the call didn't get through, the business partner called from a phone inside the office. He came out and announced to the crowd, "I left a message with the owner. When he gets it, I'm sure he'll come to straighten this out." He was too scared to resume pumping gas so just waited quietly in his car.

The people continued filling their cans as they waited for the owner to show up. Meanwhile, a portly-looking woman about fifty years of age appeared from nowhere with cups of coffee in a basket that she had purchased across the street from a Dunkin Donuts. She had seen that people were shivering from the cold wind and went down the line asking, "Who would like some hot coffee?"

Several people accepted her kind offer.

"How much do we owe you?" inquired an elderly man.

"Nothing. It's on me," she replied.

"Thank you so much and God Bless," replied a grateful woman.

Moved by her compassion, Lucas regarded the woman's effort,

then turned to his wife. "Sybil, in the midst of all this craziness, a Good Samaritan has come to visit us."

"I know," said Sybil. "I feel warm already without having to drink any coffee."

She reached for his hand and squeezed it.

As people on the line noticed her, the bickering and hostility seemed to melt away. When she ran out of coffee, she started to walk across the street to get more.

"Wait," called out Sybil, "I would like to go with you."

Others also joined her, and a group of five people went to Dunkin Donuts to purchase more coffee. They came back and distributed cups to the other people on the line. A second group followed suit and did the same thing. Within a short time, everyone in the line was offered free coffee. Lucas and Sybil had begun to lose faith in humanity as the crowd surrounded the selfish man, only to witness the kindness of the coffee messenger. Those who followed her lead were rising above all that anger.

Several minutes later, the police arrived. Apparently, someone sensing the potential for a violent confrontation, had called 911. The officers advised the young businessman to leave. They suggested if he wanted gas to return with the owner. Now that the police were in control, he left.

After almost two hours, Lucas and Sybil finally were able to get their cans filled. They carried the cans back to the car, feeling cold and exhausted. Lucas decided to put a couple of gallons in Dick's car and save the rest for the generator. In the process of putting the gas in the car, he spilled some on himself and the driveway while injuring his back. "Ouch, Christ. Nothing is easy. Can't seem to catch a break," he grumbled to himself.

In the coming days, more police officers were visible at gas stations.

With the potential for conflict high, owners began to rely on police to help with managing the long lines. To address the crisis, Governor Christie of New Jersey announced a gas rationing system based on odd/even license plate numbers, and Governor Cuomo of New York followed suit a few days later. Although that helped shorten the lines for gas, hoarding was still a problem. People got fuel every other day even though they didn't need to. The fear of not having enough gas was enough to spark this compulsive behavior.

Gina had to get back to school, but the family wasn't sure of the best way to do that. Sybil cautioned Lucas about making the long trip. "If you drive Gina back to school, I don't think you have enough gas to get back."

"I'll have to get gas in New Jersey," he said.

"That may even be harder than getting gas around here. New York City drivers are going to New Jersey to get fuel."

Gina interjected. "There are several kids in my school from Long Island. I'll text them to see how they're getting back to school."

She reached out to a few students and was able to arrange a ride with a sophomore from Suffolk County. As she was packing her things, Gina began to cry. "I don't think I can leave you guys here. You have no heat, hot water, or food. I feel like I'm abandoning you."

"Don't worry about us," Lucas replied. "Your siblings and other family members will help us. Besides, we'll feel better knowing that you are someplace safe, away from this chaos."

"We'll see you for Thanksgiving," responded Sybil, "and hopefully we'll have a new car for you to drive back to school."

When Gina's ride pulled up, they embraced their daughter. Sybil was in tears. "See you soon, sweetie. Don't worry about us. We'll call every day to let you know what's going on."

# CHAPTER 8

# SALVAGING MEMORIES

Tara had just moved into an apartment in Queens with her boyfriend Jim. Their new Ridgewood apartment suffered little damage from the storm and didn't even lose power. That was a far cry from the extensive damage that her parents had suffered in Massapequa. The house where she was born and raised was inhabitable. Tara was in daily contact with them and felt comforted that her younger sister Gina and her cadre of friends were there to help them. But Gina was on the way back to college. Tara was a teacher and had gotten word that school would be reopening on Monday. She wanted to visit her parents to help them before going back to work. As the eldest child, she felt a sense of responsibility for the well-being of her parents. Although she had a contentious relationship with them growing up, frequently fighting over curfews and freedom, she was now very close to them and even became a teacher like her mother.

Tara's drive to Massapequa was mainly uneventful until she got to the South Shore. Seeing her old elementary school with windows boarded up was painful. The courtyard where she played as a little girl during recess was now a staging area for vehicles from restoration and construction companies. Tara couldn't believe this was the same place where she had so much fun during recess. Furniture, desks, tables, computers, and office equipment had been removed from the building and were piled up throughout the teachers' parking lot. There were hoses all over the place draining seawater from the lower level of the building. This was one of the first schools built in the district. It had a proud history with some famous alumni, and Tara wondered if it would ever be the same again.

As she pulled up to the driveway of the house, her dad was taking bicycles, skiing equipment, camping gear, and golf clubs out from the garage. "Hi guys. What a relief to see that you are well!"

Her parents greeted her. She got out and gave them both a big hug and asked, "What are you doing?"

Lucas explained. "We're trying to hose down anything that can be corroded by saltwater. Our neighbors warned us that bikes, skis, and anything that has gears or other moving parts will be rotted by the salt unless they are rinsed off quickly."

"Okay, I want to help. What needs to be done first?"

"We must save the bikes," Sybil said. "I just bought mine two months ago and would hate to see it ruined. Let's get these things to the backyard so we can rinse them off."

As they proceeded to wash, clean, and dry the bikes, Tara noticed items hanging in the gazebo. "Hey mom, what's in there?"

"We put some of our damaged belongings there to dry."

As Tara walked toward the gazebo, she recognized a nauseating odor. As a teenager, she had worked one summer at a gift shop at Zach's Bay in Jones Beach State Park. Working during low tide was awful because of the repugnant odor that came from the bay. The closer she got to the gazebo, the stronger the smell. "What are all these files?" she asked her parents.

"My file cabinet was flooded," a bemoaned Lucas answered. "I had to remove all the files. Most papers were thrown out, but important documents like birth certificates, passports, the deed to the house, our will, and other legal documents, I tried to save. I'm hoping that when they dry up, they will be legible. There are also dozens of student files and teaching materials from my course at Hofstra."

"It smells awful in here," said Tara, "like dead seaweed."

Numerous pictures were clipped to a string that hung across the gazebo. Sybil had always loved photography and took many pictures of the kids when they were growing up. Quite a few were wet, and Sybil was trying to dry them.

Tara cringed. "Mom, these pictures are so badly warped, discolored, and crinkled. Do you think they're worth saving?"

"Tara, I have to save them. Four albums were damaged with pictures of when you guys were in preschool, kindergarten, and first grade." Sybil's eyes began to well with tears. "Look at these pictures of your birthday party twenty years ago at Chuck E Cheese. Your cousins and friends from the block were there."

"I remember that party," replied Tara. "And look at this picture of Greg and me." She held up a photo of her and her brother swinging baseball bats for the first time in their tee ball uniforms.

Her mother held up another photo. "This one with you and Greg holding my belly when I was pregnant with Gina is my favorite. These pictures are irreplaceable." She sobbed. "The memories are too important to me, and I don't want to lose these special moments in our lives. I'll try to restore them, but even if they can't be, we'll keep them."

"Don't be upset, Mom. My friend's uncle is a curator in a museum. Perhaps he knows someone who can help."

"Thanks, dear. I would appreciate that."

After rinsing and cleaning the items in the yard, they went inside. Tara walked around the house to inspect the damage. It was startling to see the garage, basement, and ground floor without interior walls; just the wood studs remained. "It looks like the house is being held up by large toothpicks," she remarked. "How long are these fans going to stay here? They're so loud."

"Until the studs are dry. We don't want mold. They should be gone in a day or two," replied Sybil. As Tara peeked into the office, she noticed that the aquarium was dark. "Dad, are the fish still alive?"

"I've been checking on them," replied Lucas. "Without power, the water temperature has dropped to the low sixties. For the fish to thrive, it needs to be at seventy-eight degrees. Seven have died, and there are three left. I doubt they will be alive much longer."

"I still remember when you got the tank," Tara reminisced. "I was six and Greg was five. It was so much fun the first few years. Do you remember when we dug for small worms in the ground and fed them to the fish? Greg would say that it looked like they were eating spaghetti."

"How could I forget?" Lucas said with a chuckle. "We had so much fun shopping for fish and buying accessories for the aquarium. Your favorite was Sharkfish. That guy was indestructible. He was the only one to survive after you unintentionally poured acid into the tank."

"Yes, I thought I was putting in a water clarifier," Tara recalled. "I got it mixed up with one of Mom's bathroom cleaners which had hydrochloric acid in it. Within ten minutes, all the fish were floating dead on the surface, except Sharkfish. Gina was screaming and crying. That fish was her favorite. He was nearly dead lying on the gravel at the bottom but came to life when you adjusted the PH of the water."

Lucas shook his head. "Sharkfish lived longer than any of our other fish. Nine years."

The conversation sparked some strong feeling in Tara. "Dad, I want to save these fish and bring them back to my apartment. Jim and I will take care of them until your house is livable again. We'll return them to you when that time comes."

"Okay Tara, but it's not necessary. We have more urgent things to think about."

"You're right, but this is important to me. I want to preserve part of my childhood by trying to save them. Just like mom felt such a strong connection with the pictures, I feel a connection with this aquarium."

"If you want to try, I have a small tank and fish flakes I can give you," said Lucas. ""You'll need to pick up a heater from a pet store."

They put the fish into the tank and carried them to her car. It was nice to know that a few of his tropical fish had survived the storm, and she could take them with her. Tara had bought some bagels from a shop near her home, and they took a lunch break.

"I know you guys have no food, hot water, heat, or power. How are you getting by?"

Lucas sighed. "The first couple of days we ate leftovers and canned foods. The American Red Cross came down our block and distributed packaged meals from a deli. I felt like a homeless beggar."

"Our gym reopened yesterday," said Sybil. "We went there to shower and ordered a few dinners from Ruby Tuesday. We've run out of clean clothes and need to find a place to do our laundry." She had tears in her eyes. "Since this happened, the weather has been mild enough, so we have been able to sleep under heavy blankets."

"That's about to change," Tara cautioned. "The temperature is dropping into the forties tonight. You're welcome to stay with us. We have a sofa bed in our living room."

"Thanks for the offer, dear," replied Lucas, "but I have to keep the generator going to run the refrigerator so the little food we have won't spoil. Besides, a trip to Queens means we'll be using a lot of gas."

"The gas lines are getting shorter in Queens since they started the odd/even rationing system," replied Tara. "You would be able to get gas either tonight or tomorrow. Please think about it before deciding. You've helped me out so many times when I was growing up, now it's my turn to help you."

Sybil smiled at her while Lucas walked over and kissed her forehead.

After their break, they went back to work and emptied the shed. All of Lucas's gardening supplies like fertilizers, topsoil, and seeds were contaminated by saltwater and had to be thrown out. He was able to keep his garden tools after a thorough hosing with water. By mid-afternoon, they were tired and decided to end the day.

"You should come to my apartment tonight. I won't be able to sleep worrying about you. I'll set up the extra bed in the living room," Tara pleaded.

"Okay honey, thanks for your help," replied Sybil. "I'll call you tonight to let you know."

Tara got into her car and drove away. She regretted not being more forceful. While basically healthy, her mother had high blood pressure and her father had an incident of blood clots in his lungs a few years prior. Could these medical conditions be aggravated sleeping in a cold house without heat? Tara thought of turning back to plead with them to come, but she knew it was their decision. Her father could be stubborn, and she didn't want to end her visit with an argument. She prayed that they would come to their senses and call when it became too uncomfortable.

# CHAPTER 9

# LIVING LIKE NOMADS

After Tara left, Lucas and Sybil decided to go to their gym to shower and clean up. They brought their gym bags packed with towels and a change of clothes. Sybil elected to take her swimsuit so she could relax her sore muscles in the hot tub. Lucas also brought his toiletries to shave and brush his teeth. When they arrived at the gym, Lucas went to the locker room to change, leaving his shirt, windbreaker, and towel in a locker while we went to the bathroom. When he returned minutes later, they were missing.

What happened to my things? he thought to himself. He approached several people near his locker and asked if they had seen his belongings. Lucas searched frantically for his clothes and towel but couldn't find them. He described his missing things to people in the locker room, but no one had seen them. Frustrated and extremely agitated, he went to the pool area to find Sybil, who was relaxing in the hot tub.

"Sybil, I can't believe this. Someone stole my things," shouted Lucas. "It's bad enough that our home is ruined, that our cars are lost, that the Red Cross had to feed us the other day, and we have to rely on our friends and relatives for help. Now I get ripped off by thieves."

"Lucas, calm down," said Sybil, facing him. "How do you know your things were stolen? Did you have them locked up?"

"No, I couldn't find the lock," he said in frustration. "Our house is a mess."

"Did you leave them on the bench or inside a locker?" inquired Sybil.

"A locker, I think. I'm not sure. I can't think straight."

"Is it possible that a worker saw the clothes in an open locker and removed them thinking that the owner had left? Or if you left them on the bench, someone might have taken your clothes by mistake?"

"I guess it's possible."

"And if someone did steal them, perhaps it is a person who lost everything. Just because something bad happened to us, doesn't mean we're cursed forever. We'll get over this."

Lucas hung his head and could not think of what to say. Had he overacted? These were old clothes that were not worth much. He was feeling like a victim and now acting like one. It was easy to lose perspective; no one was injured from the hurricane and the material things could be fixed or replaced. Everything seemed to be magnified after the storm. Minor life challenges that in normal times would be easy to overcome now seemed unsurmountable. While Sybil seemed logical and composed, Lucas felt angry and a bit out of control.

"Rather than pick up a meal at Ruby Tuesday, let's stay for dinner," suggested Sybil. "We need time away from the reminders of the storm. Let's talk about some fun things like places to go on our vacation next year."

Lucas tried to slow his breathing. "Sure, that makes sense to me. I need time to decompress."

When they got home, it was cold and dark. This was the first cold evening since Sandy wrecked their lives. The blankets wouldn't be sufficient to keep them warm. "Let's call Tara," advised Lucas. "We don't have to be martyrs; we have family that really care about us."

"You're right. We have always been caregivers for our children and other family members. Now we must become comfortable with receiving help."

Sybil called Tara, who was elated that her parents were coming.

When they got to her apartment, they received a warm greeting from Jim.

"I'm so glad you guys came. Tara told me about all the destruction in your home. Sorry to hear about all your pain and misery, but at least you're safe here."

"Thanks, Jim," said Lucas, "it just got too cold to stay home. I see you're taking good care of my fish."

"Yes, Tara even filled the tank with warm bottled water so they wouldn't be exposed to the chorine in tap water. She also picked up a heater in the pet store to keep the temperature at seventy-eight degrees."

"Are you guys hungry?" asked Jim.

"No thanks," replied Sybil. "We ate dinner at Ruby Tuesday. It's so great to be here in a warm place, with hot water and power."

"We haven't watched TV in nearly five days," said Lucas. "Do you mind if we put the news on to see how the recovery effort is going?"

Tara handed him the remote. "Help yourself, Dad."

Every channel was inundated with coverage of the devastation of Sandy. Progress was being made on several fronts. Most of the tunnels and train stations of the subway system in lower Manhattan, which had been flooded by a fourteen-foot storm surge, were drained of water and repairs had begun. Power had been restored to almost half of the homes affected by Sandy. There was steady progress with phone service, and most people had working phones again. Most businesses and schools were going to reopen the following week. Amidst the encouraging news was the warning that a nor'easter was going to strike early next week.

"A snowstorm in early November; that's unheard of," said Lucas.

"The poor people whose homes were completely trashed are going to face another hardship."

"How are thousands of homeless people going to survive the freezing temperatures?" said Sybil.

"The city has opened shelters for those who have no place to stay," replied Tara. "I would hope the local authorities on Long Island would do the same."

"We just can't catch a break," lamented Lucas. "First Sandy and now a snowstorm a week later. The gods must be angry at us."

Tara chuckled. "Funny to hear that from you, Dad. You're not a very religious person."

"I'm not, but I need an explanation for all this hardship."

They went to sleep fearing more trouble was on the way but enjoyed a good night's sleep in a warm bed.

The next morning, Sybil received a call from her sister, Kathy.

"Hi Sybil. I wanted you to know that we got our power back. There's a nor'easter coming, and we want you to come and stay with us for the next few days."

"That sounds good to me," she told her. "Thanks for the offer. Let me talk it over with Lucas, and I will get back to you."

Jim and Tara were wonderful hosts, but the apartment was too small for four people, so Sybil and Lucas accepted the offer.

Lucas had an appointment that day with the GEICO claims adjuster and had to drive home. Tara was right about the gas lines in Queens. He only waited about twenty minutes and got a full tank of gas. As he was driving to Massapequa, he decided to make a stop at a house he once owned with his brothers in Seaford. It was a rental property they had bought as an investment. It was located across the street from a canal. He was curious to see how it had fared during the hurricane. Lucas turned right on Neptune and passed the police station. The further he traveled south, the more damage he could see. The homes on the water were vacant with their windows boarded up.

As he turned on to Island Channel Drive, he was stunned by what he saw. A large motorboat, about twenty-five feet in length, was sitting in the middle of the street. There was a canal with a dock about sixty feet from the boat. Lucas speculated that the storm surge had lifted the boat above the dock and carried it to its present location where it was dropped once the tide changed. He had heard stories from his neighbors about boats being carried out to sea or deposited on land, but seeing it was shocking.

As he carefully drove around the boat, he saw a huge sign stretched between two poles:

LOOTERS BEWARE: TURN BACK

YOU ARE BEING WATCHED

The sign was handwritten, and he surmised that the writer was an owner of one of the vacant waterfront homes. Looting was something that he had not even considered. Why would anyone want to steal something from a home trashed by the storm? As he passed the sign, someone approached his car and demanded, "Turn around and go back. You don't live here."

"I used to own a home down here and just want to make sure the people living there are okay," explained Lucas.

"Almost all the people beyond this point have abandoned their homes," replied the stranger.

"The house is at the end of this block. I'll only be here a few minutes," pleaded Lucas.

"I'll be watching you and will call the police if you're not gone in a few minutes," the stranger warned in a threatening tone.

He felt the man's stare follow him down the block. Lucas thought about his own house, which he had abandoned the previous evening.

There were valuables such as computers, televisions, bicycles, and athletic equipment that could be easily taken. While the stranger was hostile and rude, he was protecting his property. Lucas realized he needed to be more vigilant with his own house.

When he reached his former two-family rental, the bottom windows were boarded up, and it was vacant. He tried to find a waterline on the front wall. From what he could tell, the house had been inundated with six feet of water. Across the street lived a neighbor whom he had been friendly with. Doug was in the construction business, and a work crew was gutting and rebuilding his storm-ravaged house. As he looked around at the abandoned homes, damaged bulkheads and boats, flattened fences, uprooted vegetation, and the mountain of debris brought in by the water, he wondered if this place would ever look the same again.

When he got back onto Merrick Road, he passed Cedar Creek Park where a long line of people picked up food, bottled water, blankets, and clothes from a crisis center set up by the American Red Cross. With the nor'easter coming, he wondered what would happen to these people. Would the town set up shelters as the city was doing?

Lucas reached his home and met with the GEICO claims adjuster. After a quick inspection of the three cars, the adjuster declared, "I am going to label all three cars as a total loss."

"My car is only three months old," replied Lucas. "There is no way it can be repaired?"

"No, once the engine is penetrated by salt water, it's ruined. You will be reimbursed for the book value of the cars."

Lucas was upset. "The value of my almost-new car will be several thousand less than what I bought it for."

"There is nothing I can do about that," said the adjuster with a stoic demeanor. "That's how these claims are calculated."

It was starting to dawn on Lucas that while replacing the cars was going to be a huge expense, they were only a piece of a much larger picture. Fixing the house, restoring the outside property, and replacing all that was lost inside the house was going to be the biggest financial challenge they had ever faced. He worried that while insurance would help cover some of these losses, it was clear that much of the costs they would have to pay.

As the adjuster was finishing the paperwork, Lucas asked, "When will you be able to tow these cars away? They're a painful reminder of all that we have been through."

"Because there are thousands of cars that need to be carted away, it may take a few weeks," he replied.

As Lucas was getting prepared to leave, the warning sign he had seen for looters and the hostile man he encountered concerned him. He made sure that all the doors were locked but could do nothing about the garage door, which had been pushed in by the storm. There was enough space for someone to crawl underneath and get into the house. With no walls in the lower levels, they could easily get into any room. Lucas moved his work bench and blocked the opening. It wasn't much for a barricade, but it was the best he could do.

His next stop would be Kathy and Todd's house where he would be meeting up with Sybil. The couple was very gracious to invite them and sleeping in an actual bedroom was appealing. He feared the nor'easter that was coming, but at least he would be with family.

# CHAPTER 10

## MAKING PROGRESS

Lucas arrived at Kathy and Todd's home in the early evening and found Sybil doing laundry. "Can you add my clothes to your pile?" he asked.

"You can, but I'm not going to get them right away," replied Sybil. "I've already done two washes, and I have several more to do. It's the first time I'm doing laundry since that horrible day. It's a nice feeling to have clean clothes again."

"I also brought a suit for a workshop I'm doing tomorrow morning at St. John's University," said Lucas.

"Do you expect people to show up?" asked Sybil.

"Well, the coordinator hasn't cancelled it, so I'm going to proceed as if it's still on."

Kathy had ordered food at a deli, and the four of them had a nice dinner. Their hosts were gracious and kind. They talked about happier times. After dinner, Lucas and Sybil watched some sitcoms on TV and went to bed at eleven. It seemed like the typical evening that they had experienced countless times before Sandy. It was nice to experience normalcy for one evening.

The next morning, Lucas began to prepare for his workshop at St. John's University. It had been almost three years since he had retired from his position as a school administrator for the Massapequa School District and had started working as an adjunct professor at Hofstra University. His main assignment was teaching a graduate course on bereavement counseling to students in the school counseling program. He was giving a workshop that morning on gender differences in grief to facilitators of bereavement support groups. Lucas had given this workshop before, so he just needed to quickly review his notes from previous presentations. The coordinator of the conference, Fr. O'Reilly, had emailed him the day before confirming that it was on. He got dressed and was about to leave when he received a call.

It was Father O'Reilly. "I hope I caught you in time."

"Yes, I was just leaving the house."

"Good, I'm glad you didn't get on the road yet. We have had many cancellations this morning. People are calling and saying that they are having transportation problems. Since much of the subway system is still out, many more people are driving, causing all kinds of congestion, and you know about the long lines to get gas."

"Sounds like people waited till the last minute. Poor planning, I guess," surmised Lucas.

"There may be more to it than that," replied Fr. O'Reilly. "I don't think people are in the right frame of mind. They're focused on day-to-day hardships and on restoring their lives after the storm. We have a lot of traumatized people out there who are barely functioning. Tomorrow's New York City marathon has been cancelled, which has added to this feeling of gloom."

"I agree with you, Father, and with this nor'easter coming, people are more demoralized than ever," confirmed Lucas. "Who can think about attending a conference during such stressful times?"

"I will try to reschedule the conference for next month. When I have a better idea of what's going on, I'll call you." With that, Fr. O'Reilly hung up.

Although Lucas was looking forward to doing the workshop as a distraction from all his worries, he wasn't disappointed that the event was being postponed. This wasn't a good time for professional development; storm victims had to tend to their basic needs.

Sybil wanted to use the weekend to find a new car. She was using her father's car, but it was time to return it. GEICO was reimbursing her about two-thirds of the value of the Nissan Rogue that she had lost. Her options were limited; there were few used cars available, so she was forced to go to a new car dealer. Because of supply and demand, the dealers had the upper hand on the thousands of customers looking to buy or lease a car.

Sybil had done research in consumer magazines and knew what car she wanted. After a long wait, a salesperson finally became available.

"Hi, how can I help you?" said a young man.

"I am looking for a Mazda CX5. Do you have any on your lot?" she asked.

"We have several. Let's take a look at our inventory and see if there is anything you like."

After several minutes of walking and inspecting each car, she said, "None of these cars have the features that I'm looking for. They seem to be very basic models with few upgrades."

"That's all that we have left on our lot. If you want a more customized CX5 with specific upgrades, it may take a few weeks to get one. Supply is tight right now, and we may have to order from Mazda dealers down south or the Midwest."

"I don't have that kind of time," replied Sybil. "I'm going back to work on Wednesday, and I need a car. The asking price for these cars seems rather high."

"Make me an offer," said the salesperson, "and I will check with my manager."

Sybil was great at negotiating for cars. Perhaps it was the teacher in her, but she was adept at wearing down salesmen. Lucas often brought her along when shopping for a car. However, she had no time to play the back-and-forth dance that often accompanies a sale and was in a weak bargaining position, so she offered a modest reduction of five hundred from the asking price.

After checking with his manager, he said, "Sorry, Miss, but he will only sell it for the asking price."

"That's nuts," replied Sybil. "Car prices are always negotiable."

"That's usually the case, but not now," said the salesperson. "There are many buyers and not enough cars."

Sybil didn't want to spend the day going to different car dealers. With a shortage of cars, chances were that other automobile dealers would give her the same treatment. She leased one of the cars on the lot and wanted to know if it could be ready the next day.

"Ordinarily we could, but because of the gasoline shortage, it may take until Tuesday."

An exasperated Sybil replied, "Please be sure it's ready. I must get to work. Call me if there's a problem."

The young man assured her the car would be ready.

No sooner had she hung up than Lucas called her to let her know that he'd gotten a call from a FEMA inspector who wanted to meet with them to give an estimate on the damage to the house. Sybil, still aggravated over her failed negotiations over the car, perked up. It would be an important step forward. The inspector's report would tell them how much they could expect to be reimbursed so the couple would know how much money they'd have to rebuild. She shared her excitement with Lucas that they would soon have the green light to begin contacting contractors and start getting estimates.

Suddenly things were looking up, and hope was replacing frustration. With some luck, repairs could begin before Thanksgiving, and they could have their house fixed by Christmas. It was always their tradition to host a big holiday dinner for the whole family, one they couldn't miss, even on account of a storm like this.

"I'm starting to see the light at the end of the tunnel," proclaimed Sybil. They hugged each other with the optimism that things were finally moving forward.

# CHAPTER 11

# THE INSPECTOR

When Lucas and Sybil pulled up to their house, the inspector from FEMA was already there. The tall African American man introduced himself with a southern accent, "Hello, I'm Franklyn Holly from FEMA."

Lucas shook his hand. "Nice to meet you. We have been looking forward to this meeting."

At the sight of their ravaged home, he said ruefully, "Wow, I can see that you have been through a lot. Sorry for all your troubles."

"Thank you, I hope you haven't been waiting long."

"No, not a problem. I got here early," replied the inspector. "I wasn't sure how long it would take to get here from New Haven, so I gave myself more time than I needed."

"You're coming from Connecticut?" said Lucas. "Aren't there FEMA offices in New York?"

"Actually, I'm coming from Alabama," replied the inspector. "I was going to take a flight to JFK but couldn't get a hotel room on Long Island. Every hotel room was booked. I had to fly to Hartford and stayed at a Best Western in New Haven."

"So where are the local inspectors?" interjected Sybil.

"They're all on jobs, ma'am. All of us from the Northeast, Midwest, and South have been called in to help. We have over one hundred thousand claims on Long Island alone."

As they entered the house, Sybil exchanged a look with Lucas, and they both knew what the other was thinking. Were they assigned someone with limited experience because FEMA was overextended? Did this inspector even know the cost of living, or how expensive construction was in this area?

"Have you done many hurricane damage appraisals?" Lucas asked Mr. Holly.

"Yes sir, where I'm from we often get flood claims in the spring when the Mississippi overflows its banks. Sometimes entire towns are flooded with water."

"This is different because we're dealing with salt water," replied Lucas.

"We take that into consideration," said Mr. Holly. "Besides, I've done claims for homeowners on the Gulf as well."

Lucas turned his attention to the skeletal remains of the ground floor. "As you can see, we removed all the Sheetrock from the walls the day after the storm to prevent mold."

"That's fine as long as you didn't begin repairs," said the inspector. "Sometimes people do that, and it complicates the process. The wood studs look dry to me. You can get rid of all these fans."

He took out a measuring tape and began recording where the water level reached in each room. "I hope you understand that your FEMA flood policy only covers structural damage to the home. Things like the washer and dryer, oil burner, air conditioning, refrigerator, and water pump are not covered."

Sybil leaned back, blindsided. "No, we didn't know that," she said with tension in her voice. "Replacing even one of those items is going to be expensive. Is there any way to recoup them?"

"Claim them on your federal and state tax returns as uninsured losses. You can also file for a reassessment with the county tax department for a reduction in your property taxes since your home is worth a lot less now. I don't know how things work here, but some state and town governments have funds for disaster relief. Call them and see if they have any that you qualify for. Any damage to the outside of the house?"

As they walked outside, Lucas pointed to the front of the house and noted several items. "My garage door was pushed in, and part of it was lifted off the ground. We also lost roof shingles and gutters, and some windows were damaged."

"We'll cover the garage door, but those other things are related to wind damage. You should file a claim with your homeowner's insurance for them." He looked at the foundation of the house which stood two feet above ground. "It doesn't look like the storm surge shifted the house from its foundation. That's good news. Your house is still stable."

Lucas was surprised. "A storm surge can actually lift a house from its foundation?"

"Oh yes. Older homes are not attached to the foundation. The house sits on it, and if flood waters are deep enough and moving fast, it can cause the house to shift. In extreme cases, it can pull the house off the foundation. We see that a lot with oceanfront homes. Huge waves during a storm can knock the house off its foundation. I have seen some homes that were separated from their foundation by forty feet."

Lucas shook his head in disbelief. "I'd hate to see what that storm looked like."

Mr. Holly glanced at the backyard. "So many of your plants, scrubs, and trees have been uprooted."

"Yeah, I don't think they're salvageable," said Lucas. "My gardener is going to replace them."

"Sir, you may want to wait at least six months or even a year before you put in new plants and trees. The ground right now is saturated with salt. If you plant new shrubs too soon, the salt will be absorbed by the roots and it will kill them. If you wait, the rain will gradually wash the salt out of the top layers of soil."

"While I'd hate to leave the backyard looking like this over the spring and summer," Lucas said, "you make a good point."

"The same applies to your garden. Don't expect to be able to grow vegetables this summer. The soil will be too acidic. Bring the PH down before you resume with your garden," suggested Mr. Holly.

"Thanks for the advice. I might rent a plot from a community garden next summer."

They went back into the house, and the inspector started to calculate all the damage that he observed to the garage, basement, and ground floor. After several minutes of inputting numbers into his computer, he declared, "By my calculations, you will need $61,000 to repair this home."

"Wow, I'm surprised," said Sybil. "Some of my neighbors on the same side of the block just had their estimates done, and their figures were in the $75,000 to $80,000 range."

"That is true. While every home on this block was exposed to a flood level that reached four feet, the damage to each home can vary," explained the inspector. "There are factors that can limit the damage. Imagine if this door to the garage and the one to the yard hadn't held out. If they busted open, you would have had a wave of water entering your house that would have done even more damage."

"Did you factor in cost of living?" Sybil countered. "It's very expensive to live in this part of the country and repairing a home here would be more costly than in Alabama."

Mr. Holly smiled reassuringly. "Yes ma'am, we use this manual that gives us regional differences in prices of construction materials." He showed Lucas and Sybil charts from the book depicting the varying prices across the country. "If you aren't happy with my report, there is an appeal process. Homeowners must write a letter to FEMA and explain to them why the amount of the assistance being offered is insufficient. You have sixty days to decide if you want to file an appeal."

"And how long will that take?" Lucas inquired.

"I'm not sure," replied the inspector. "But given all the claims we're working on, it may take months."

"No, we want to move forward with fixing the house," said Lucas. "When can we expect to get the check for these repairs?"

"After I submit the paperwork this week, it may take up to about two months."

"What?" protested Sybil. "That's crazy. We can't live with this for two more months."

"You can apply for a disaster loan from the Small Business Administration," said Mr. Holly. "You would get a better interest rate than going to a bank."

The couple thanked Mr. Holly for all the information he provided and escorted him to the front door.

After he was gone, Sybil faced Lucas with downcast eyes "Well, that was a rude awakening. Do you think we should write an appeal letter?"

"I don't think so. It sounds like a long process," he answered. "Besides, Mr. Holly seemed very knowledgeable and thorough. There's no guarantee we'll get more money and don't want to waste our time. We just have to figure out how we are going to pay for it."

"Well, I don't want to take a loan out. Even if the SBA is offering a good rate, we have to pay it back with interest," she said. "We have a home equity line of credit on the house. Let's use it."

"We can do that and pay off the balance when we start getting checks from GEICO, FEMA, and our homeowners insurance policy for the wind damage."

"Well, we can pay off some of the balance," clarified Sybil. "Even with our insurance coverage: fixing the house, buying new cars, repairing the oil burner, water pump, and air conditioner, and replacing the washer and dryer is going to cost a tremendous amount of money."

He nodded. "And when you factor in all the furniture and electronic equipment we lost as well as the outside property damage that needs restoration, we are going to face a huge debt, maybe $100,000 or more by the time we are done."

"All the more reason to follow up with some of the inspector's suggestions," said Sybil. "I'll call the county tax department tomorrow to see how we can file for a reduction in our property taxes, and maybe you can reach out to the Town of Oyster Bay to see if there are any disaster relief programs available."

"That makes sense," replied Lucas. "We can also start calling contractors for estimates so we can get moving on repairs. I'd like to see how much $61,000 will buy us. Maybe we can cut out some things that aren't essential."

They got into the car and began driving back to Kathy and Todd's house. While relieved they had a better idea of what needed to be done on the road to recovery, the meeting with the inspector left them feeling anxious and preoccupied. How would they manage this huge mountain of debt that was coming? Would they have to use their retirement savings, or withdraw money from Gina's college savings account? They hoped not, but realized it was a strong possibility. Was there no end to this debacle? The costs seemed endless.

## CHAPTER 12

# ELECTION DAY

On November 6, in the midst of the shock, anguish, and ruin of post-Sandy Long Island, one of the most tightly contested elections in modern US history was taking place. Polls had President Barack Obama and challenger Mitt Romney in a statistical tie going into election day. Lucas was a lifelong Democrat who always voted on election day.

As they woke up and started to plan their day, Lucas turned to his wife. "With all the storm damage, I'm not sure what to expect at our polling place. We might have to wait in line for a while."

"Tara told me the elementary school where we usually vote was flooded," Sybil said. "We may not be able to vote there."

He waved her off. "Our right to vote is sacred, and I'm sure there must be some way to vote today."

They drove to the site where they had always voted and found the school in complete disarray. The school had been thrashed by Sandy, and it was closed. A crew of the construction workers were busy working to get it reopened. Lucas asked a worker, "Do you know where we go to vote today?" The worker shook his head. "Not here. The voting machines in the basement were flooded."

"What about the other schools in the district?" Lucas asked.

"I don't know, but none of the schools have power yet."

Sybil piped up. "Let's check Newsday. They've been giving us updates on the recovery effort and services for storm victims. Today's edition should be at our front door by now."

When they got home, the paper was one of few services that

were working just as before. The paper had arrived and listed all the polling places where they could go. They chose Plainedge High School in North Massapequa since it was the closest. But when they arrived, the line was long.

"This is going to take forever," complained Lucas.

"Give them a chance, Lucas," she replied. "They seem very organized."

When it was finally their turn to vote, one of the poll workers, an elderly man sitting behind the table, asked for their name and address.

"We don't live in this community," Lucas said.

"You have to complete a provisional ballot," the man explained.

"What's that?" asked Sybil.

"We have no way of verifying your identity. Provide all the information on the ballot, and once we verify it your vote will be accepted."

"We live south of Merrick Road, and our entire community was under water," explained Lucas. "Almost no one has power, and most public offices are closed. How are you going to verify our information by the time the polls close?"

With the people on the long line getting antsy, the elderly man stood up. "Sir, the election monitors can verify after 9 p.m. There are thousands of people in your situation. They have a process in place to get it done."

"Well, we're staying with relatives half an hour from here," said Sybil. "We've driven a long way and just want to make sure our votes will count."

"There is a procedure in place." He spoke as if reciting from a script. "You just have to trust the system and follow the directions that I am giving you."

Sensing that the poll worker was getting annoyed, they completed the provisional ballots and gave them to him.

"How is this election going to be valid if displaced people like us don't even know if our votes will count?" muttered Lucas.

"Let's go back to Kathy and Todd's house," said Sybil. "There's nothing more they can do for us here. We'll just have to trust that the system works."

Lucas thought for a moment. "It just occurred to me that Sandy not only disrupted the lives of millions of people, but a weather event might also impact the outcome of a presidential election. That's got to be a first in US politics."

That evening, Lucas drove back to his home. Still concerned about looting, he thought his daily visits would be a deterrent to unscrupulous individuals. Getting gas for his neighbor's generators was also important since that was part of their agreement. While Lucas no longer lived there, Sam made frequent visits to his home and needed power because he was doing some of the repairs on his own. He had also begun meeting with contractors from construction companies.

As Lucas drove to Massapequa, he saw signs of recovery. The street and traffic lights were working on Merrick Road and to the north of it. But when he turned south, it was like entering the netherworld. Everything was completely dark. All the streetlights were out, and the homes had little or no light. It made the moon and stars more visible in the sky. The only sound he could hear were the rattling of generators. Collectively, they were like a band of poorly tuned instruments producing a cacophony of discordant melodies. It was eerie, like entering the set of a horror movie.

Lucas pulled up to his house and went to the backyard to put gas in the generator. The air seemed turbulent that night with swirling winds and the clouds were moving fast across the sky. The nor'easter was supposed to reach Long Island the following day, so he assumed that the unsettled weather was a preview of what was about to come. After adding fuel, he started the generator, which gave him light in his study. Lucas proceeded to call contractors to schedule visits. His calls mainly reached answering machines. Frustration set in as he realized that they were probably out giving estimates to others. "Here we go again," he mumbled to himself. "Every time I'm ready to move forward, I always hit a barrier."

In this post-Sandy world, everything seemed to involve a long wait. It was another case of supply and demand: too many homeowners who needed repairs and not enough contractors. The wood studs were dry now, so Lucas moved all the fans to the garage and left a phone message with the restoration company to pick them up. When he was done, he turned on the radio to listen to the results of the election.

The polls had closed in most parts of the country, and results were starting to come in.

Lucas was surprised to hear that Obama was leading in almost all the states that he had won in 2008. The pundits had predicted that the election would be a toss-up, but that was not what was happening.

He decided to call a friend, Ronnie, who was a history teacher in a school where he had worked. No one knew more about politics and current events than Ronnie. They were both progressive Democrats and had participated in anti-war demonstrations during the Iraq war.

"I heard that Massapequa was hit hard by the storm," Ronnie said on the call. "Are you guys okay?"

"Fortunately, no one was injured, but the storm surge flooded our home and the entire community."

"How are you managing?"

"It's been a nightmare. My house is a wreck, and we have been living with relatives.

We're trying to make the best of it, but progress has been slow. Are you following the election results?"

"Yeah, I'm watching the results now," said Ronnie. "Were you able to vote?"

"I couldn't vote at my school," answered Lucas. "I had to go to a neighboring school district and fill out a provisional ballot. I hope my vote will count."

"A lot of people had to do that, Lucas. It's a standard procedure. You should be fine."

"I thought this was supposed to be a close race, but Obama is clearly winning. What happened?" asked Lucas.

"It appears that Sandy may have actually helped Obama. Polls show that over 60 percent of people surveyed approved of his leadership in the aftermath of the storm. Only 18 percent disapproved."

"Yeah, I saw news reports of Obama visiting New Jersey after declaring it a disaster area," responded Lucas. The Republicans were furious with Governor Christie for shaking hands with Obama. It was all over the news. On the eve of the election, getting that kind of reception from a Republican governor made Obama look good."

"That's the way it should be. During times like this, people need to put their differences aside and work together. But I think Sandy helped Obama in another way as well," added Ronnie.

"How's that?"

"The disruption created by the storm changed the momentum of the race. Going into the last week of the campaign, it seemed that Romney was even or pulling ahead of Obama, but the storm changed everything. Over eight million people lost power, and hundreds of thousands like yourself were flooded and suddenly had no place to live. How could victims think about an election when they have no power? They need to keep warm and figure out where their next meal is coming from."

"I see what you're saying, Ronnie. I certainly haven't been thinking about politics these days. Maybe Sandy was a Democrat," joked Lucas. They both laughed.

As they continued to follow the results, Ronnie and Lucas cheered when Obama was declared the winner by the Associated Press.

"Mr. Hope and Change prevailed again," declared Lucas.

Ronnie was exuberant. "What a great night for the middle class!"

After Romney's concession speech, they ended the call. It was late, and Lucas didn't want to drive back to his in-laws. He called his wife.

"Honey, I'm going to sleep here tonight."

"Are you crazy, Lucas? The temperature will be dropping into the thirties."

"Yeah, but I'm tired, and I don't want to fall asleep at the wheel."

"Well, if you're staying, at least use the extra blankets in the linen closet. And those hand warmers we have from all those skiing trips," Sybil advised.

"Okay, I'll do that. See you tomorrow morning."

"Make sure you leave early, dear. There's another storm coming midday," cautioned Sybil. "We also have to pick up the new car."

"Don't worry. I'll be there early to needle Todd over the results of the election," he chuckled.

In what had been one of the worst weeks of his life, Lucas went to sleep that night with a smile on his face. He climbed into a freezing cold bed with hand warmers underneath him. Finally, some good news, he thought. Our first African American president has been re-elected.

# CHAPTER 13

# THE NOR'EASTER

Sybil was visiting with her parents, anxiously waiting for Lucas to arrive so they could go pick her new car. "Thanks for letting us use your car mom. We couldn't have gotten by without it."

"You're welcome, dear. Glad we were able to help," replied Sharon.

As soon saw Lucas pulled up to the front of the building, Sybil went outside to meet him.

"How did you sleep last night?" She embraced him. "It was so cold."

"The extra blankets and hand warmers helped," he replied.

"Now it's my time to drive. Let's go pick up my car!" she said excitedly.

Sybil drove her father's car one last time to the Mazda dealership to pick up her new vehicle. The salesman made good on his assurance to have the car ready with a tank full of gas so she could go back to work the next day.

"It's great to have my own car again. I feel like a part of me has been restored. Now let's return my parents' car."

"Don't feel so relieved. We still have to get a car for Gina and one for me," Lucas reminded her, frustration deep in his voice. "I can't get a new car for Gina without going into our college savings."

"We may be better off getting a used car for her," replied Sybil. "It will cost less, and she can get a new car when she graduates. Bart has a brother-in-law who sells used cars. Maybe he has some for you to look at by now."

Lucas and Sybil would spend another day at Kathy's house. As they arrived, they noticed Todd collecting snow shovels, brushes, a bucket of sand, and a snow blower.

"Hey Todd, getting ready for another storm?" asked Lucas.

"Yep," replied Todd. "After the debacle with Sandy, I want to make sure I'm prepared for this nor'easter."

"I'm supposed to go back to work tomorrow," added Sybil. "It's hard to believe that we are having a snowstorm the first week of November. This is like the sequel to a horror movie."

"We've got to get all the paraphernalia ready," continued Todd. "I must make sure this snow blower is working."

After pulling the throttle several times, Todd noticed that the fuel gage was on empty. "Damn it. Now what? We're supposed to get a lot of snow."

"Don't worry," said Lucas. "I have a gas can in my car. I'll head to a gas station and fill it up."

"You can't," said Sybil. "My license plate ends in an even number, and today is for odd-numbered plates."

"Just drop me off the block before the gas station, and I'll walk up to the pump," said Lucas. "The attendant won't even know."

Sybil drove by the gas station where she saw a line several blocks long of people waiting to fill their cars or gas cans. "It looks like everybody had the same idea."

Lucas sighed. "The last time we had a line like this, we waited for two hours. It's way too cold to wait that long. I'll have to try again in the morning. At least I can drive there since it'll be an even-numbered day."

They drove back to Kathy's house with the bad news.

"No problem," Todd assured them. "We have four sets of hands to shovel your car out in the morning. We'll be fine."

As they went to sleep that evening, Lucas and Sybil prepared themselves for another bout with Mother Nature. They were awakened the next morning by a phone call from Sybil's principal, Gary.

Lucas noticed that his wife was very animated and agitated on the phone. As soon as the call was over, he asked, "what was that about?"

"There is no school today. The school buses can't pick up the students because of the slick roads and some of the schools lost power again." She paced across the room. "I was looking forward to going back to work. What a terrible time for a snow day," she complained. "School should reopen tomorrow, but Gary said that we've already missed eight days and the school board is thinking about canceling vacation days to make up for lost time. What a mess!"

"Okay but there is a silver lining here, You don't have to drive your new car in bad weather and we could use your help to shovel the snow."

"That's true, I guess I am overreacting. Why is it so chilly in here?" she said, shivering. "I can almost see my breath."

No heat was coming up from the radiator. They walked to the window and pulled up the blinds. Peering through the frosted glass, the couple could see nearly a foot of snow was already blanketing the ground.

"Looks like we've got a lot of work to do," said Sybil. "Let's go downstairs and see what happened to the heat."

In the kitchen, they saw Kathy and Todd warming up by the stove. "Why is it is so cold in here?" Sybil asked.

"We lost power again last night," said Kathy. "I heard on the radio that tens of thousands of people who recently got power back are in the dark again."

"Was it that windy?" asked Sybil.

"Wind gusts reached fifty to sixty miles an hour. They had to shut down the Long Island Railroad since several trees fell down on its tracks," replied Kathy.

"I can't go to work today," added Todd. "It's going to take the maintenance crew several hours to clear the tracks. Most of the power outages were from the wet, heavy snow. You got all these weak cables, then the trees collapse on them, and they're done for."

"At least the gas stove is working, and we can stay in the kitchen," said Kathy.

Todd shook his head in defeat. "You can't get gas for the snow blower, Lucas. Not until we clear the driveway so we can get the cars out. We'll have to do this by hand."

As the four of them went outside with shovels in hand, they were awed by what they saw. "Look down the block," said Lucas. "It's truly breathtaking."

The virgin white snow drooped on the trees. Because of the time of year, many of them still had leaves, and the wet snow clung to them. The leaves, branches, and trunks were barely visible under a brilliant white covering. Icicles hung from electric cables suspended on telephone poles and from the gutters of homes. It appeared to be a winter fantasy, like a page from a children's book on some winter fable.

Sybil thought of the beautiful morning after Sandy. "It's amazing that after Mother Nature shows us her power and destruction, she also reminds us that nothing can match her beauty."

The other three marveled in agreement.

Removing the wet snow was a real challenge. The slush made the snow heavy, and they strained their backs lifting it. The four worked slowly in clearing the driveway and a path to the front door. When they finished, Lucas went to get gas. He encountered a long line again, but this time he was in Sybil's new car where it was warm, and he could play music. After filling up the gas can, he returned to the house. Todd filled the fuel tank of the snow blower and finished clearing his property.

After the cleanup, the weary sisters and their husbands put the snow gear away and gathered in the kitchen. Kathy made some hot chocolate, and they ate lunch while pondering their next move.

"We'll be okay during the day," began Kathy. "But if the power's not back by evening, we won't be able to stay here tonight. The temperature is below freezing, and the bedrooms will be too cold."

"We can try to get a hotel room," suggested Todd.

"There aren't any available," said Lucas. "The FEMA inspector who came to our house had to stay in a hotel in Connecticut because nothing was available on Long Island."

"What about Debbie?" said Todd. "Does she have power?"

"Not since this morning," said Kathy. "Besides, I don't think our sister has room for all of us. She has some friends staying over whose homes were also flooded by Sandy."

"Well, Mom and Dad still have power in their apartment."

"But their apartment is so small," said Kathy. "Where would we all sleep?"

"We have several inflatable mattresses that our kids used years ago when they had sleepovers," said Sybil. "I saw them when we cleared out the shed. They were on the top shelf, and the floodwaters didn't reach them."

"We could pick them up from our house and meet you at their apartment," suggested Lucas.

"I'm not so sure about that," cautioned Kathy. "You know how neurotic they get when they have company. How are they going to feel about putting us up overnight?"

"They were great about lending us their car," countered Sybil. "While a bit cranky at times, they love us and have always made sacrifices for their children. I remember plenty of times in your teenage years, Kathy, when you came in late and drunk. Dad always hollered and threatened punishment, but after a day or so all was forgiven."

"Well, you never did anything wrong," countered Kathy. "You were the obedient daughter, conscientious student, and a school cheerleader, so how would you know?"

"Let's not relive family wars," said Todd. "I see no harm in asking them. We don't have many good options, and I'd rather not spend the night in a shelter for storm victims."

"If we don't get power by sunset, I'll call Mom," said Sybil. "I'll tell her about the air mattresses, and that we'll sleep on the living room floor to keep things neat and not intrude on their privacy."

By 6 p.m., power hadn't returned, so Sybil called her parents.

"Hi Mom. We're at Kathy and Todd's. They don't have power, and we have no place to stay tonight."

"Come and stay with us," replied Sharon.

"Are you sure? Is Dad okay with the four of us coming?"

"He's right here nodding his head. Please come."

"Great. We have air mattresses and will sleep on the floor," offered Sybil. "We'll be there in a couple of hours."

When they arrived, Dick and Sharon greeted them with a table full of refreshments, including wine, cheese, and crackers.

"We thought that you might not have had dinner, so we prepared some food for you," said Dick.

Sybil glowed. "What a treat! Thank you."

They toasted to better times ahead. Sybil could tell that something was up with her sister. She had a frown on her face and was tapping the floor with her foot. Was Kathy looking for redemption after what she said about her adolescence? After their toast, Kathy spoke up.

"Sybil thinks that I was a difficult teenager. Was I that bad?"

"Well," started Dick. "Let's just say that there was never a dull moment when you were growing up." They all chuckled.

"Dad was the enforcer," explained Sybil. "But he was rarely home, so we ran circles around Mom."

"We did what we wanted and even got Mom to write notes to the teacher when we didn't finish our homework or were going to be late to school," added Kathy.

"I think you girls are imagining things," said Sharon sheepishly. "I always checked your schoolwork, and if you misbehaved, you were sent to your room."

"Yes, and I spent the night talking on the phone with my friends or watching TV," Kathy said with a laugh.

"You and Debbie also tortured me with our stupid dog and spiteful cat," said Sybil. She turned to Todd and Lucas. "They were animal lovers. They knew that I was afraid of them, so they would put them under my covers while I was sleeping to scare me."

"And it worked every time," gloated Kathy. "She'd wake up screaming."

The evening was filled with many such stories as the they laughed and drank plenty of wine.

"I wonder if what we're doing is happening in many families tonight," said Sybil.

"What do you mean?" asked Sharon.

"By coming together and reminiscing about our family, we're also reconnecting."

Dick interjected. "That's a good point. During good times, it is easy to drift apart with our busy lives, but during tough times when we have power outages, gas shortages, and people without a home, families find a way to come together."

"Sandy brought us a lot of hardship," said Lucas. "But I bet she brought many families closer together who had to rely on one another for help."

"Mom and Dad," said Sybil. "I have to say, we weren't sure how you would respond to us coming here tonight. We've underestimated you guys too many times. You made us feel so welcome, and the warm hospitality is much appreciated. All joking aside, you are great parents."

"Thanks, dear," said Dick, tearing up. "Let's make one final toast before going to bed: To Sandy for helping us rediscover the meaning of family."

# CHAPTER 14

# REMOVING AND REBUILDING

The power outages caused by the nor'easter were short-lived. For Todd and Kathy, and most of the other neighbors, power was restored within a couple of days. Lucas and Sybil, on the other hand, were among the thousands south of Merrick Road who would remain in the dark for many days to come. Lucas finally got some return calls from contractors, and he made appointments with them to get estimates on the cost of repairing the house. He scheduled these meetings on the same day that a tow truck was coming to take his flooded vehicles away.

"They're finally removing these rusting metal corpses from the front of our house," he told Sybil.

She sighed with relief. "I'll be so glad to see them gone. Every time I see them, I'm reminded of the awful day."

Lucas's face was drawn. "When I look at my Ford Edge, I have flashbacks of the car filling up with water that night at the intersection. I was terrified that I wouldn't make it back to the house."

A huge two-tier tow truck pulled up in front of the house and a large, bearded man dressed in overalls came out. He looked like a lumberjack without an axe. Lucas and Sybil came out to greet him. He said hello and handed them forms to sign.

"You lost three cars! Sorry to hear that."

"Thank you," said Lucas. "Where will they be taken?"

"Flooded cars are being taken to holding areas all over Long Island," explained the driver. "There are too many to dispose of, so they'll have to wait in these lots until we can get to them. These are going to Nickerson Beach State Park with hundreds of others."

"Where do they go from there?" said Sybil.

"Most will be crushed and carted to recycling centers."

"What a waste," replied Lucas. "Nothing from these cars can be salvaged?"

"It depends," said the driver. "Sometimes parts of the car can be reused, but with flooded cars the metallic and electronic components will corrode. Little is worth saving, but some do reappear months later."

"What do you mean by that?" asked Lucas.

"People steal them from the lots; they fix the cars, dry and clean them, and sell them as used vehicles."

"Wow, that's outrageous," answered Sybil. "Buyers can't tell that a car was flooded?"

"If the thieves clean it up and deodorize well enough, they can get away with it. Especially if the price is right."

"I don't understand," said Lucas. "How can these cars function when they were submerged in salt water?"

"They take them apart, remove as much sand and water as possible, and put them back together. The car can work fine for a while, but when the corrosion sets in the engine and transmission, it eventually breaks down. There are dishonest people in this world who look for opportunities to profit from a situation like this."

The driver loaded the first car. A large hook with a chain was placed under the car, and a motor pulled it onto the top tier. He repeated the process with the other two cars, pulling them onto the lower tier. "Good riddance," shouted Lucas. They leaned on each other and watched as the truck pulled away, three entire vehicles now gone from their driveway.

"We just turned one more page in this terrible chapter of our lives," said Lucas. She nodded in agreement.

Sybil strode over to the driveway and scanned the now-empty driveway before them. "We have so much more room now. Lucas, I'm ready to meet our first contractor. How did you find him?"

"He's a well-known local guy with a fine reputation who has done a lot of work in the community."

"We must try to stay within the limit of the FEMA reimbursement," reasoned Sybil. "From what I've heard, most of them try to persuade you to renovate more than you need so they can make the most money, but then you wind up paying a lot of money out of your own pocket."

Lucas rolled his eyes. "Don't be so cynical. There are honest people in this world, and we need to be open minded."

<hr>

They had some time before the first appointment, so they took notes on the repairs they needed and questions to ask. A middle-aged, well-built man with a military style crew cut stepped out of an old Volvo van and announced his arrival. "Hi, I'm Harry. You called me for an estimate on your home."

Lucas shook his hand and introduced himself and his wife. "Thanks for coming, Harry. We had a damage estimate from a FEMA inspector, and our aim is to repair the home within the amount of money we're getting from our claim."

"I don't know what they're offering you, but I will try to get your home repaired as economical as possible," assured the contractor.

Harry toured the house with them, scribbling in his notebook and sharing his observations. The first few renovations would be easy. The walls had to be sheetrocked and spackled, so there wasn't much to discuss. The more discretionary items required some discourse.

"What do you want to do with your floor?" asked Harry. "Several tiles came up, and others are cracked."

"Yes, the refrigerator fell on them," said Lucas.

"I can replace them, but the new tiles are not going to match your floor."

"Well, I don't want the replacement tiles to stand out and make the floor look like a patched-up job," replied Sybil.

"Then I advise you to replace the floor."

While they did want to repair the house as economically as possible, Lucas reasoned that the house must look presentable.

They agreed to replace the floor.

"What do you want to do with the cabinets in the bar area?" asked Harry. "The bottom cabinets were immersed in water, and it looks like the wood is already beginning to warp. They need to be replaced, but I'm not able to match them with cabinets above the sink."

"I want the cabinets to match," Sybil insisted.

"To do that, I will have to replace them all," Harry replied.

"Okay, what about the doors on this floor?" inquired Lucas. "Can we just paint them?"

The contractor stood up and examined each door. "They don't close properly. They must be pushed hard to close them. Exposure to salt water has caused them to swell, and now they don't fit right."

"Well, if these two doors need to be replaced, I want the other doors replaced as well," said Sybil. "The doors should all be the same type."

"The bottom of our garage door was pushed in by the storm surge," noted Lucas. "Can it be banged out?"

"You can, but it's not going to look right," said Harry. "Once metal is dented to that extent, it will never be smooth again. It's going to appear like it was damaged. Besides, when you get power back, it may not open and close properly. I suggest you get a new one."

Lucas folded his arms on his chest and began pacing around the room, sensing that the total cost would far exceed his expectations. Almost every renovation involved the same discussion. Fixing something didn't mean that is would look right or work as well as before. They seemed to do a lot more replacing than repairing. Finally, when the entire job was reviewed, they were given an estimate of $85,000.

That can't be," he protested. "That is $24,000 more than what FEMA is giving us."

Henry patiently explained to them the reality of the predicament. "You have to understand that the inspector gave you an appraisal based on what it would cost to repair your house, not what it would cost to restore it to its original condition. It's a matter of functionality versus aesthetics."

"I understand the difference," replied Sybil. "Harry, we're going to think about your suggestions and get some other estimates. You have been very thorough, and we appreciate your time."

As Harry left, she turned to Lucas. "I don't want to live in a house that looks patched up. If we must go into debt to make it look right, that's what we have to do. We can file an appeal with FEMA to see if they will give us more money."

With his head hanging low, he agreed. "The house must look pleasing to us. How are we going to entertain or have visitors if our house is embarrassing?"

Throughout the next few days, they met with three other estimators. When deciding what needed to be repaired, the same issues surfaced. Their estimates were similar, varying by a few thousand dollars. It was a choice between being cost-effective or doing it right. Lucas and Sybil wanted the latter and knew they would have to pay the price.

The last contractor was unexpected. Someone knocked on the door. When Lucas answered, a Hispanic man in his twenties said, "Hi mista, my name is Rodrigo. I'm going up and down your block to see if people need repairs on their home."

"Actually, I've been meeting with contractors to get estimates," replied Lucas. Looking for a truck or commercial van, he didn't see anything and asked, "Who do you work for?"

"I work in Queens and use my own car," said Rodrigo. "I fix walls that need sheetrock and spackling. When I saw on the news all the homes that were broken by the storm, I came here to see if anyone wanted to hire me to fix them."

Lucas had heard that many people outside the county were coming to communities damaged by Sandy to find work. He was curious to see what kind of estimate he would get. "Come in and let me show you what needs to be done." And let's see if you can save me some money, he added silently.

The young contractor took out a tape measure and proceeded to measure all the walls that needed work. He took out a notepad and did some calculations. "Mista, I can fix all these walls for $12,000. We do only walls, so you will have to get someone else to fix the floor, cabinets, and the other things."

"That's about half the price that the others are charging me," replied Lucas. "Are you using good quality materials?"

"Yes Mista, I use the same materials," answered Rodrigo. "I don't hire workers. My brothers and I do all the work, and we have few expenses."

If Lucas hired him to work on the walls and got someone else to do the rest, he could bring his total cost down by $12,000.

"Wow, you have given me some things to think about. Let me

discuss this with my wife and I'll get back to you."

When eating dinner that night, he told Sybil about the unexpected visitor and his offer.

"That doesn't sound right," she said. "How can he do the same work using the same materials for so much less?"

"There you go being cynical again. My guess is that they are poor immigrants who are willing to charge less to get the job," said Lucas.

"What if they're undocumented?" said Sybil. "They could start the job and disappear if someone reports them to ICE, and I doubt they have insurance."

"We would be taking a risk. But I bet they would do a good job. Our landscapers are such hardworking people. They work for less money and never complain."

"I don't want to take any chances. Besides, we should give our local contractors the work to help the community."

"I'd like to check with an old friend before making a decision. His knowledge of home construction is impressive, and he also knows a lot of the local people in the home renovation business."

Sybil threw up her hands. "Fine with me. But do it soon so we can hire someone. Tomorrow is my first day of work in almost two weeks. I'm looking forward to having a routine again."

"Since you'll have the car all day tomorrow, maybe I'll sleep here tonight. You can stay at your sister's house, and I'll see my friend in the morning."

Lucas readied himself for another lonely, cold night with a radio and flashlight, but he was feeling better and more hopeful that there was an end in sight to this awful experience.

# CHAPTER 15

# THE PEOPLE WHO LOST THEIR HOMES

Lucas woke up the following morning shivering. His hands felt like ice. He decided to walk to Merrick Road to pick up coffee at Dunkin' Donuts. His buddy Peter's house was on the way, so he planned to stop by to see him. They had worked together at Massapequa High School as administrators for five years and developed a good relationship. Lucas and Peter shared many common interests such as biking, skiing, and politics, and when they retired became close friends. Peter started his career as an industrial arts shop teacher and knew a lot about construction. Lucas often consulted with him when he was planning a house project. He had no contact with Peter since the storm and was happy to see his friend when he arrived at his house. The difference was astounding—Peter's house was untouched by the storm. Lucas gave Peter a big hug.

"Lucas, I've been thinking about you," said Peter. "I ran into Sybil a few days after Sandy, and she told me all about the damage you suffered."

"Yes, it's been horrible," replied Lucas. "We've been staying with my sister-in-law, and I came here during the day to meet contractors to get estimates on the house. Hopefully, we can start to rebuild soon. What about you?"

"We were lucky. Since our house is farther north, we didn't get the water damage that you did. But my daughter Marie's house is a few blocks from you."

"Yes, I know her house is two blocks east of ours. How did she make out?"

"Her house was ruined." Pete began to choke up, his voice quivering. "She has a small ranch near Ocean Avenue, and every room was inundated with water. With colonials, high ranches, and splits, the owners were spared damage to the upper levels, but with ranch homes they were completely decimated."

"Sorry to hear that," said Lucas. "Is she okay?"

"Physically she's fine, but very distraught."

"She wasn't home that evening, I hope?"

"No, Marie was with us that night, and she and the baby have been with us ever since."

Lucas smiled at the news. "Every time I see a ranch house, especially one that has only one or two front steps, I pray that the people weren't in their home that night. We were able to escape the flood waters by moving upstairs. They would have had no place to go." He shuddered. "I heard that some homes actually caught fire."

Peter nodded. "That's what happened in Breezy Point, Queens. Some people there still had power during Sandy, and when water from the storm surge met the electricity, it started a fire. With the strong winds fueling it, the fire spread to other homes and several blocks burned down."

Lucas gasped. "That must have been like a scene from a movie with water flooding the lower parts of the homes and fire burning the upper parts. That's a good reminder that, as bad as we had it, some people had it much worse. It's amazing that more people didn't die."

"Most of those communities on the beach like Far Rockaway and Breezy were evacuated by firefighters and police," said Peter. "Otherwise, there would have been many more fatalities."

"Is Marie having the house repaired?"

"We've been getting estimates, but I wonder if it's worth

repairing. Every room has to be redone," lamented Peter. "The kitchen was especially hit hard, and an oil leak from the burner left oil throughout the house. Every estimate has been over $100,000."

"Did you get an appraisal from Harry's company?" asked Lucas.

"Yes, it was similar to the others. Are you thinking of using him?"

"Possibly. Do you know anything about the company?"

Peter nodded. "Harry has been around a long time, and I know him. His company renovated my bathroom several years ago. They're not cheap, but I was happy with their work."

"Well, an endorsement from you means a lot to me," replied Lucas. "I had this young Latino man from Queens offer to do the sheetrock and spackling for half the price of the others."

"That's because there are no overhead costs. They don't have a company and are working on the side. If you don't like the quality of the work, there is no project manager or supervisor to complain to. I prefer experience and someone I know."

"You sound like my wife," Lucas remarked. "Very logical and risk-averse. You guys have me outnumbered, so I guess I'll use Harry's company. Thanks for the feedback."

After their visit, Lucas called Harry and made arrangements to sign the contract. Harry assured him that the work would begin right after Thanksgiving and be completed in January.

When Lucas returned home, he saw his neighbor, Barry, sitting on the front steps of his house. He was such a lonely figure in that moment, bent over and staring at a letter he had just opened. Lucas walked toward him.

"Hey Barry, I haven't seen you in a while. What's going on?"

"Hi Lucas. Barbara and I have been staying with my son in Westchester County."

"How did you get here?" asked Lucas. "Did your son drive you?"

"No, I came on my own. I finally got a check from the insurance company for the two cars we lost during Sandy, and I bought a used car to get here."

"We're staying with my in-laws," added Lucas. "But I just signed a contract with a construction company and hopefully will begin rebuilding soon. How's it going with repairing your house?"

"I'm nowhere," replied a dejected Barry. "I applied for a grant from FEMA and just learned they'll only give me $11,000."

"Don't you have flood insurance?"

"No. when I paid off my house, I didn't renew it. That was a big mistake on my part," admitted Barry. "The repair estimates on my house are $95,000 to $100,000. No way am I going to be able to pay that."

"Why so high? Our estimates were lower."

"It took me a few days to arrange for someone to drain the water from my house. These flood management companies were really backed up, and I wasn't around." Barry sighed. "By the time I was able to get someone, I had a serious mold infestation throughout the house. I would have to spend several thousand dollars to treat the mold before the workers can begin working on the house. That has ballooned the total cost of fixing my house. I still have wet walls and furniture that need to be removed."

"What about taking out a loan?" said Lucas. "We've been putting all of our expenses on a home equity line of credit. This gives us several years to repay our debts."

Barry shook his head. "Five years ago, my hardware store went out of business, and I had to declare bankruptcy. I might be able to get a small loan from the Small Business Administration, but I couldn't get a large, affordable loan from a bank because of my credit rating."

"I heard Obama is proposing a large relief bill to Congress, about sixty billion," noted Lucas. "I'm sure there will be some money for homeowners."

"My understanding is that the money is going to the cities and local governments to repair infrastructure, schools, and buildings. Even if there is money for homeowners, it will take months to get through Congress. I don't have that kind of time."

"Perhaps the state or HUD has some programs that can help," suggested Lucas.

"I have done a lot of research," said Barry, his voice cracking. "And there is nothing that can help me now. My last hope is to try to get a reverse mortgage, and I don't know if a bank will give me one with the house in such terrible condition. Other than that, I don't see any solutions that would buy me the time I need to hold on to my house. A builder approached me yesterday who wants to buy my house. He would knock it down and build a new, larger house."

"Barry, don't do it," Lucas warned. "There are a lot of vultures out there looking to profit from the misfortune of others. He'll offer you a ridiculously low price because he knows you're desperate."

Barry trembled. "I don't want to leave this house. I've been living here for fifty years and love this place, but at seventy-seven, my age has caught up to me. I'm too tired and don't have the energy to fight any longer. I was hoping that FEMA would help me, but what they're offering is far less than I need. Getting a reverse mortgage is my last hope. There are no options left, and the stress is killing me. If I must sell the house, I could rent an apartment and start over."

"What does your wife want to do?"

Barry was visibly upset and fighting back tears. "She would like to stay as well, but Barbara is so upset that she can't sleep at night. It's difficult living with my son; they have two small children, and we're sleeping in their beds while they sleep on the floor. We feel like an intrusion on their lives, and she won't stay there much longer."

"I wish I had other ideas, suggestions, or words of wisdom, but I don't," Lucas said with his arm around his shoulder. "We have known each other for over thirty years, and I have enjoyed being your neighbor. I have always admired your character and sense of optimism. It pains me to see you like this."

"I appreciate the kind words, and I will not give up without a fight," said Barry, sobbing. "I intend to leave no stone unturned to save my house, and if you can think of anything else, please let me know."

Lucas was struggling to think of something to say. Words that would lift his spirits and give him hope but nothing came out. He wanted to somehow rescue his friend but realized he could not. Barry was a shell of his former self. His tall frame was sitting in a crouched position, looking helpless and defeated. Not having any more to say, Lucas just embraced the man and held him in his arms.

"Barry, just know that whatever happens, you will always be an icon to me. You are the last of the original homeowners, and we have nothing but fond memories of you and Barbara."

"Thanks, Lucas," replied Barry. "I will always remember your support and friendship."

# CHAPTER 16

# THE GOOD, THE BAD, AND THE UGLY

After being out of work for nearly two weeks, Sybil wanted her first day back to go smoothly. She got up early, showered, and dressed. As she walked down the stairs, she smelled the wonderful aroma of bacon cooking on the stove. Kathy had decided to treat her to a nice breakfast of bacon and eggs to start her day.

"You look great, Sybil," said her sister.

Sybil blushed. "Thanks. I really needed some affirmation so I could feel like myself again. I appreciate the nice breakfast. Thanks for everything."

Kathy smiled at her. "I just wanted to make sure your day got off to a good start."

Sybil smiled. "Yes, and you've succeeded." She sat down at the table. "It feels like I've been away so long from my colleagues and students."

"That's because so much has happened to you since you were last there," said Kathy.

"Teaching high school math is challenging under normal circumstances," Sybil replied. "But after the shock of Sandy and living in limbo all these days, I have to get my mind refocused on teaching geometry."

"Just follow your routine," advised Kathy. "Go through the steps that you normally take to get ready for your classes. That will get you in the right frame of mind to take on the day."

"That makes sense to me," Sybil said in between bites of bacon. "I'll put my teacher hat on and let my instincts take over."

After quickly finishing her breakfast, she grabbed her car keys and briefcase, hardly believing it was already time to go to work again.

Kathy wished her luck on her first day back. "I look forward to hearing about it at dinner."

On her drive to work, Sybil reflected for a moment on what Kathy said, but already the daily routine was not the same. She encountered light traffic; some schools and businesses still hadn't reopened yet. It was great having a new car, but she had to park on the street since her space in the faculty lot was occupied by snow mounds from the nor'easter. She signed in at the front office where the principal's secretary greeted her.

"Welcome back, Sybil. Are you okay? We heard you were homeless."

"Well, not quite. We're staying with my sister," she said.

"What was it like being trapped in your house while it was filling up with water?"

"It was awful. I've got to get to ready for my first class. We'll talk later."

Sybil knew that there would be many conversations like that one. It was a small high school, and after working there for over twenty years, everybody knew her. Bad news spread very quickly among the staff and students. When she got to her classroom, Sybil started writing a "do now" problem and placed it on an overhead projector. It was her way of getting the students focused on the lesson as soon as they walked in. One of her more talkative students, Miguel, came up to her.

"Mrs. S, we were worried about you. We heard your father had to come to rescue you from the roof of your house."

"No, I think you're getting Sandy mixed up with Hurricane Katrina," she said, trying hard not to laugh. "We just borrowed his car after the storm because we lost ours."

"How many cars did you lose?"

"Three. Thanks for your concern, but please have a seat and start working on the problem."

At her lunch break, she sat with three other math teachers in the faculty lounge.

"Sybil, why didn't you evacuate your home?" asked Kate, the AP Calculus teacher.

"I listened to my husband," Sybil said while shaking her head. "I should have known better. He thought the weather forecasters were exaggerating the severity of the storm."

"How did you escape?" asked Betty, a special education teacher.

"We stayed in the house and just moved upstairs; the storm surge never reached the upper floors."

Her friends were enthralled with the details of how they fought to keep the water out of the house. Her student teacher, Joan, asked, "A friend of mine said fish actually came into her house with the water. Did any come in your house?"

"No, but after his car stalled, Lucas did almost step on a furry animal walking back to the house," she said flippantly.

These interactions went on all day as teachers and students approached her to express their concern, sympathy, and curiosity for all that she had been through. Other teachers also had no power and experienced damage to their homes from falling tree limbs, but they were still in their homes. None were living like nomads because their house was inhabitable. They meant well, and she was appreciative of their support, but it was exhausting answering all their questions. A department meeting was planned after school to discuss how the teachers were going to make up all the instructional time that was lost.

The math department chair Alex Napa began the meeting by welcoming everyone back and reviewing items from the agenda he had distributed. He was very formal and meticulous in his presentation. Near the end of the meeting, Sybil's lunch buddy, Betty, stood up and asked her to come to the front of the room. Sybil stared at her with a puzzled look on her face.

Betty gestured toward her coworker. "Sybil, we know that you have been through a lot, and we wanted to do something to help you in recovering from this terrible ordeal. It is a small token of our love and concern for you." She handed her an envelope.

Sybil's eyes opened wide, her mouth was agape, and she felt her face turning red. Hesitating, not knowing what to say, she finally spoke with a trembling voice, "I am humbled by your kindness." Her eyes filled by with tears. "I have always enjoyed our friendship, and while this was unexpected and unnecessary, your support is very touching. I have a lot of bad memories since that night, but this act of generosity I will remember most."

Each teacher gave her a hug and whispered kind things to her. In the midst of one of the darkest chapters in her life, the goodness of people brought light into her world and lifted her spirit.

***

After Lucas signed the contract with Harry, his next task was to get Gina a replacement for her Honda Civic. He had assured Gina that he would have a car for her when she returned for Thanksgiving. His wife had suggested that he go through Bart, the owner of a Mobil station on Merrick Road. He had serviced their cars through the years and was highly regarded by his customers. Lucas walked to the station and found him working on the engine of a Chevy pickup truck.

"Hi Bart. I want to thank you for being so helpful to us after the storm. Sybil told me you sold her gas before the scheduled time, so she didn't have to wait on a long line."

"You're welcome," he replied while putting down the wrench to face Lucas. "I try to show my customers the same loyalty they show me. Did she get a new car?"

"Yes, she just got it yesterday, but now I'm here for my daughter. Sybil tells me that you also sell used cars."

"That's right. I showcase them on the lot next door, and my brother-in-law, Darryl, does the actual business transaction."

"She told me you have a few cars that Gina would like. She was driving a Honda Civic. Do you have anything comparable?"

"Well, I have a Honda Accord, which is a bigger, more solid car."

He walked over to show the car to Lucas. It was a beige four-door sedan with a sunroof. Lucas carefully inspected the car, and the stylish body was in mint condition. He thought to himself, I could see Gina in this car.

"It costs more but gives you a much better ride," added Bart.

"I know this car has an excellent reputation for reliability" said Lucas. "It is an upgrade over the Civic, and I like the standard features, plus it has a few extras like the sunroof. What is the year and mileage?"

"It's a 2009 and has 35,000 miles."

"Hmm, it may need new tires soon." Lucas dropped to one knee to look at them. "How much do you want for it?"

"I'm not sure, since Darryl handles the business end, but my guess is about $17,000."

Lucas was hoping to get something for much less, so he wouldn't have to use the college savings that he had set aside for Gina. However, he wanted her to drive a quality car with good reliability. Lucas decided to spend the extra money even if it meant Gina might have to take out a student loan for her last year of college.

"I'll take the car. How do I arrange a meeting with Darryl?"

"He works out of a car dealership in Syosset. I'll let you use the vehicle as a loaner car. This way you can test drive it on your way there."

"That works for me."

He started the Accord and drove off. It had a six-cylinder engine with good acceleration and had a nimble feel when turning. The engine was a bit noisy, something that would bother an older person like himself, but not a college student. Besides, he thought to himself, she'll love the sunroof in the nice weather. When he got to the dealership, he met with Darryl, a very friendly, sharply dressed man with a perfectly trimmed beard. Darryl was already arranging the paperwork to be signed. Lucas saw that the price of the car was listed as $19,500 on the contract. "Bart said the price of the car would be about $17,000," he said.

"This car has many upgrades," replied Darryl. "It's one of the best used cars we have on the lot, and it will sell quickly. Besides, it's Honda certified, which is factored into the price."

Lucas wasn't even sure what Honda certified meant, but he trusted Bart and didn't think this loyal mechanic would do business with a crooked brother-in-law. He wrote a check from the college savings account, signed the contract, and drove the Accord to West Hempstead to spend the evening with Sybil, Kathy, and Todd.

As they sat for dinner, Sybil spoke about her first day back at work and the wonderful gift she had received from the teachers in her department.

"$420 to help us rebuild. I have already set it aside toward a new washer and dryer."

"That's amazing," said Kathy, "What a compassionate group!"

"Lucas, I see you bought a Honda Accord for Gina," said Sybil.

"It rides really nice, and I think she'll like it," Lucas said with confidence. "The car is a big improvement over the Civic."

"What did you pay for it?"

He looked up and said, "I spent more than I wanted to—$19,500—but I think it is the right car for Gina.

"That sounds like a lot for an almost four-year-old Accord with 35,000 miles on it," said Todd. "A new one goes for about $26,000."

"He made it sound like a good deal because it's Honda certified."

"That means that the car was thoroughly inspected and that you get an extended warranty on certain parts like the power train," Todd explained.

Lucas stared in space for a minute. "Are you sure?"

"Yes, I'm positive. It's a standard line Honda salespeople use to make you think you're something special."

Lucas paused, then said sheepishly, "Sounds like I got taken. Maybe he sensed my urgency and assumed I would go along with an inflated price."

"I'm surprised," said Sybil. "You're usually very circumspect when it comes to buying a car."

"I know I usually research the consumer magazines and look online for car ratings. But I became complacent and got lulled into thinking that because Bart was trustworthy, I would get a good deal from a relative."

"Why would someone take advantage of a storm victim?" said Kathy.

"To make money," Todd replied. "The same reason why gas prices are going up and store items are more expensive."

"I feel bad for Gina," Lucas said with remorse. "She is the one who ultimately will be paying for my bad judgment."

For the rest of dinner, he silently picked at the food on his plate.

——◆——

Gina was a nursing student at a state college in New Jersey. As an out-of-state student, she paid double the tuition that in-state residents paid. Even though his family income was too high to qualify, Lucas applied for financial aid each year. As a former high school counselor who did college advising, he knew that a college would reconsider financial aid if a family's financial circumstances had changed during that school year. In a phone call with Gina, she shared some interesting news with him.

"Hey Dad, some of my friends received some grant money from the college because Sandy damaged or destroyed their homes. Why don't you apply?"

"Thanks for letting me know," replied Lucas. "I was thinking of writing a letter to their financial aid office. Now I definitely will."

Lucas saw this as an opportunity to help Gina. Because of all the losses they suffered from the storm, Gina would have to get loans to pay for her last year of college. If he could get some financial aid, he would use that money towards her tuition for senior year and perhaps she wouldn't need to take out a loan.

In his letter to the financial aid office, he explained all the damages they had suffered and included copies of forms he received from FEMA and other insurance companies to support his claim. He faxed it to the office so that it would arrive as expeditiously as possible. After waiting several days and not getting a response, he became impatient and called the office.

"Hi, I'm calling because I faxed you an appeal letter requesting that my financial aid package for my daughter Gina to be reconsidered since I suffered extensive damage from Hurricane Sandy. I sent it over a week ago and have not heard anything. Did you receive it?"

"Hold on and let me check," replied the office worker. After a few minutes, she came back on. "Yes, I found your letter. Sorry for the delay, but because she is an out-of-state student, the process is taking longer."

"How much longer before I get a response?"

"It will be soon. We will begin processing out-of-state students tomorrow."

As he hung up the phone, Lucas wondered why students living in a different state were being processed after in-state students. He was uneasy and suspicious about it all.

The day before Thanksgiving, Lucas got up early and drove to New Jersey to pick up Gina for the holiday. Since he still had not heard from the financial aid office, he was going to drop in and give them additional documentation to support his claim. When he got to Gina's dorm, he greeted her with a big hug. "Hi sweetie, it's great to see you. What are all these boxes and suitcases? It feels like you're moving out again."

She laughed. "No, Dad, this is the season where I pack all my fall clothes and bring them home to make room for my winter clothes. I'm looking forward to being with you guys this Thanksgiving, especially with all that has happened. I feel like I've been away for so long, and it's only been three weeks."

"I feel that way too," agreed Lucas. "Time has been moving in slow motion since Sandy."

"Have you made progress with fixing the house?"

Lucas shrugged. "Not much. We hired a contractor, but he hasn't started working on it yet. It looks pretty much the same as the day you left. We did make progress with the cars. Mom has a new car, and I bought you one last week, which I drove here to pick you up."

"Oh great! I heard from Mom that you bought me a Honda Accord."

"Yes, it rides really nicely, and I think you'll enjoy it." Lucas sighed. "But I had to use the money I saved for your last year of college. We have so much debt that you're probably going have to take out a student loan for senior year."

Gina could see how bad he felt. "Don't worry about that. Some of my friends had to take out loans for all four years of college, so one year isn't such a big deal." She smiled and gave him a heartfelt hug. "Did you hear from the financial aid office? My friends already received awards. Their tuition was discounted for the spring semester."

"They haven't gotten back to me, but I had planned to stop by today to see what's going on. Check out your car and take it for a ride." Lucas handed her the key. "I don't expect to be long, since the campus is emptying out for the holiday."

Lucas walked into the office and requested to see a financial aid counselor. He was greeted by a young man who looked almost the same age as Gina.

"Hello, I'm Ray Hardy. How can I help you?"

"I wrote a letter to this office a couple of weeks ago," explained Lucas. "I sustained extensive damage during the hurricane, and I'm asking that my 2012/2013 financial aid package be re-evaluated since my financial circumstances have changed. I brought some additional documents with me to verify my losses."

The young man checked his computer. "We reviewed your file, and I'm sorry to say that you weren't awarded any additional aid."

"Why not?" protested Lucas. "My daughter has several friends who were storm victims and they received discounted tuition for the spring semester."

"I can't discuss with you the circumstances of other students. That's confidential," replied the counselor.

Lucas could feel his blood pressure rising, and he was losing his civility. He stared into the young man's eyes, and with an indignant voice said, "I demand to know why my daughter didn't receive the same consideration as other the students."

"I am not sure the reason, but I will check with my supervisor," said the young man and left the office.

The director of financial aid, an older gentleman with a very officious air, came in and said, "Sir, you weren't awarded aid for storm damage because there is none left. The state did provide us with emergency funds to repair the campus and help students whose families sustained losses, but the stipulation was that New Jersey students would get priority."

Lucas was stunned. With a fierce look in his eyes, he said, "My daughter pays twice the tuition that in-state students pay and should receive the same treatment."

His shoulders slumped, and with a contrite tone in his voice said, "I know that it doesn't seem fair, but we have to follow the criteria set by the state. New Jersey got hit just as hard as the city and Long Island. Hundreds of claims were filed, and we couldn't help everyone. The money came from New Jersey taxpayers. Perhaps you can see if New York State can help you."

"My daughter doesn't attend a New York State school, so they would have no reason to help her." Lucas's voice resonated and grew louder. "She is a student at your school, and you're discriminating against her because she doesn't live in New Jersey."

"Sorry, but the funds are gone," replied the director, and left.

Lucas stormed out of the office and screamed "bastard" when he got outside. He was about to make an ugly scene; he felt like he was about to explode. First, he was taken advantage of by a used car dealer, and now the school was denying him aid that they awarded to other students. He was trembling with rage and wanted to punch something. He then saw Gina showing off her new car to some friends. She was so excited as she drove them around with the sunroof down. Seeing her happy suddenly drained all the anger out of his body. He thought to himself, If I made her happy, isn't that all that matters?

"Hey Gina," he shouted. "Looks like you're having fun."

"I am," she replied. "I love this car, and my friends do too. Big improvement over the Civic. Thanks for buying it. Can I drive it home?"

"Sure," Lucas said, feeling composed and relieved once again. He got into the passenger side, and she drove to Massapequa.

# CHAPTER 17

# POWER IS RESTORED

Two and a half weeks into the power outage, the residents south of Merrick Road were getting quite antsy. Power had been restored to 90 percent of Long Island, but the homeowners who suffered the most damage were still in the dark. West End Avenue resembled a ghost town as the colder weather forced many to stay away. As Lucas arrived mid-morning to check on the house, he missed the normal smells of people cooking and the chatter of families in their homes. Instead, there was a noxious odor of burning fuel and the loud, incessant clanging of generators from the few residents who remained.

Lucas and Sybil's next-door neighbor, Sam, worked on his deck with his father-in-law, Frank, who was a supervisor for the county. Lucas knew Frank as a friendly, outgoing, and somewhat pompous individual who loved to boast about how well the Town of Oyster served its residents. Now was a good opportunity to find out if the town was doing its job.

Sam held a fallen post against the deck while Frank hammered it in.

"Hi Frank," Lucas greeted him. "We're going on three weeks without power. Some of the neighbors and I have called the electric company, and no one seems to be getting through to them. We leave messages and never get a reply. Is the county getting involved in this?"

Frank put the hammer down and stood up. "Yes, it's been difficult getting through to them. There are five vacancies on the board of LIPA that the governor was supposed to fill, and one of them was the communication chief, so the company has no leader to inform residents and give accurate progress reports on repairs."

Lucas huffed. "Okay, that explains why they aren't calling back. But what's taking so long to restore power? I was reading in the newspaper that hundreds of utility workers from power companies outside the state were brought in to help out."

"Yes, that's true, but when the workers arrived, they found an antiquated computer system that kept breaking down. They had to resort to maps to find the problem spots, but those maps were often inaccurate, and that caused further delays. The National Grid workers who maintain the system couldn't read the maps either."

Lucas let out a deep sigh. "I get that there are a lot of problems with LIPA, but the town should be overseeing its response to the storm. They aren't accountable to voters, but the town is."

Frank ignored Lucas at first and resumed working on the deck. When he saw that Lucas was not going away, he took a deep breath and tried to explain further. "Like I said, the governor was negligent for not filling board vacancies, and the county government is responsible for dealing with the power company, not the individual towns."

"That's not helping us," interjected Sam. "We haven't had power for weeks, and people are tired of living this way. The town should be able to do something."

"Pointing fingers is not going to fix the problem," added Lucas. "We need action."

"I'll check with the town official who is working with LIPA and get back to both of you," assured Frank.

Lucas thanked him but walked away dissatisfied. He was convinced that Frank and his town cronies were not doing enough. It was obvious to him that the town officials should demand a meeting with LIPA executives and hold them accountable. If he didn't get a positive response from Frank, he would consider getting Newsday involved. Criticism of the town for their lack of response in the mostly widely read newspaper on the Island might finally get these guys to do their jobs.

Lucas got a call from Frank the next day. He informed Lucas that a LIPA inspector was visiting each home explaining to residents what they would have to do before the power was turned on. Lucas thanked him for his help. It seemed his persistence had made a difference.

Later that day, someone knocked on the door, and a man dressed in a uniform with a LIPA hat greeted him.

"Hi sir, are you the owner of this home?"

"Yes," replied Lucas.

"I'm from LIPA and just wanted to let you know that we are planning to restore power this week. But before we can proceed, we must make sure that homeowners have made the necessary repairs to the electrical system of their home."

"Sure, just let me know what needs to be done." Lucas let him in.

The inspector walked through the house with him, noting every electric power issue. "The outlets in your basement and ground floor that were submerged in water must be repaired by an electrician. Damaged wiring can cause short circuits and start fires when power is restored. Was your main electrical panel flooded?"

"I'm not sure. It's in the garage," replied Lucas.

When they entered the garage, the inspector looked at the panel. "It doesn't look like the water reached that high, but your oil burner is pretty low and was probably flooded. You may want to call your oil company to check it out. We can restore power to your system, but you won't get any heat or hot water if the burner isn't working."

Lucas took careful notes. After the inspector left, he called the contractor.

"Hey Harry, I got wonderful news today. We're getting power back, but I need an electrician to repair outlets that were flooded."

"They're all out on jobs today," Harry replied, "But I'll see if I can get someone over there later in the week."

He then called his oil company to request a technician to service his burner. The operator explained that workers weren't making maintenance visits until the power was restored.

"How will I know if the burner is working?" asked Lucas. "If it's not, we'll be without heat and hot water."

"We have too many customers requesting service visits," said the operator. "When power is restored, we'll come to those who need repairs."

Lucas couldn't win that argument and ended the call. He took a closer look at the burner. The electrical component was near the top of the unit, so it may have escaped damage.

By Thursday, the outlets had been repaired and the electrical panel was fine. Everything was ready for power to be restored. An electrician came to certify that the homes on the block were ready for power. Those that still needed work weren't approved. Lucas's house passed inspection. Both he and Sybil began pumping their fists and cheering over having electricity again. "Tomorrow morning, you'll get your power back," said the electrician.

"Do we need to do anything?" said Sybil.

"All your switches should be on the off position except one light. When that light comes on, appliances, computers, and televisions should be plugged in gradually so that the incoming energy doesn't overwhelm your electrical system and trip the circuit breakers."

The next day, nineteen days after the storm, Lucas and Sybil anxiously waited for the light to come on. Sybil put a hand to his shoulder. "What is the first thing you're going to do when we get power back?"

He trembled with anticipation. "I want to take a hot shower. I'm so tired of showering at the gym and your sister's house. What about you?"

"I want to turn up the thermostat and get some heat in here. And I want to watch my favorite TV shows."

The moment finally arrived when the light in his study lit up. He plugged in all the electrical cords and went around the house putting on all the light switches, then the kitchen appliances, the computers, and television. Everything worked, but the most important was yet to come. He stepped into the garage with fingers crossed and plugged in the oil burner. They waited patiently, but it never ignited.

"Damn Slomin's!" shouted Lucas. "Plenty of our neighbors were able to get their oil company to replace the electrical component, but ours refused."

Lucas got on the phone and called them. He had to restrain himself and spoke slowly.

"Hello, miss, I spoke to you last week. We got power back this morning and the burner isn't working. I wish you would have taken care of it then."

"Not a problem," replied the woman. "We'll have a service technician out there on Monday."

"Not a problem for you," he said shouting into the phone. "But this means we won't have heat or hot water for three more days."

"Sorry, but it is the earliest we can get there." She hung up.

"Lucas, there's nothing we can do," said Sybil. "Let's not make ourselves crazy. We've lived with this for nineteen days. What's another three days?"

"But where do we sleep tonight?" said Lucas. "Todd and Sharon have been very hospitable, but I just want to sleep in our own bed."

She put her arms around him. "Me too. We still have plenty of hand warmers that we can put around our bed, and the temperature tonight will be in the high forties, so we can manage, but I do plan on getting my second wish."

"What was that again?"

"I want to watch our favorite television program."

They set up two folding chairs in their family room, propped up the flat screen TV on a step stool, and leaned it against the wood studs of the wall.

"This seems rather silly," said Lucas, "but I could use some laughs."

They watched several reruns of Everyone Loves Raymond.

# CHAPTER 18

# UNSEEN LOOTERS

Since Lucas saw the warning sign on looting in Seaford shortly after the storm, he was apprehensive about leaving his home unattended at night. It would have been easy for someone to come through the garage or ground floor and steal computers, televisions, printers, and other valuables. Ironically, that kind of looting wasn't common or widespread in most communities damaged by Sandy. However, there was plenty of looting that took place under the guise of normal and legal business transactions. On the surface, there was no criminal activity taking place, but many people were profiting at the expense of the victims.

After spending a nice Thanksgiving with her extended family, Sybil received a call from a project manager who worked for Harry's company. He wanted to meet with them to review the reconstruction of the bottom two floors of their house. They agreed to meet the next day.

The following afternoon a tall, middle-aged man showed up at their door. He had steely blue eyes with gray hair and was physically fit. His name was Lenny and he would be the foreman responsible for the project. "I just wanted to go over with the two of you the steps we will take in the rebuilding of your house and answer any questions that you may have."

"That's awesome," said Sybil. "Please come in. Let's sit at our kitchen table and go over your plans. When are you starting?"

"We will start on Monday," replied Lenny. "We'll begin by sheetrocking and repairing the walls. Then the crew will work from the bottom up starting with the ceiling and cedar closet in the basement." They then walked down to the ground floor. Pointing to the bathroom, Lenny said, "We'll replace the vanity, tiles, and shower. Next will be the bar where we replace the cabinets, and sink." Walking to the other side where the study was located, he motioned with his hand. "All of this needs a complete overhaul. We will rebuild your study and put built-in bookcases. Finally, we'll install the floor tiles. We do that last so you won't have to worry about traffic from the workers scratching up the new floor."

"That sounds like a good plan," Lucas said with enthusiasm.

"The order of the project makes sense to me," agreed Sybil. "When do you expect to finish?"

"By the end of January, early February at the latest," replied Lenny.

After he left, Lucas turned to his wife. "Lenny obviously has a lot of experience and seems to know what he is doing."

Sybil nodded. "I like his plan. It's very organized and methodical. Also, starting with the basement makes sense. The workers will be working on one room at a time, so the dirt and dust will be confined to one room rather than the entire floor."

With Lenny in charge, they felt optimistic about the outcome of the project. They looked forward to having their house repaired before spring so they could enjoy the nice weather and concentrate on restoring the outside of their property.

<hr/>

On Monday morning, a crew of workers deposited a dumpster in front of their house. They dismantled the bar and bathroom, discarding all the material in the dumpster, and then unloaded a large delivery of Sheetrock into the garage. By the end of the day, most of the basement had been repaired. Sybil went out to pick out new cabinets and bathroom tiles, while Lucas looked for floor tiles and furniture for his office. In less than week, the workers had repaired the walls. Lenny came every day to check that the work was done properly. On his last visit, he informed the homeowners about a problem with the plumbing. "There's a leak in the pipe that drains the toilet and connects with the sewer line outside. A plumber has to fix it before the workers can continue with the project."

"Is that going to delay the completion of the job?" she asked.

"Not really. It should be done in less than a day," he assured her.

A week passed without any work being done on the house. The bathroom tiles, cabinets, vanity, doors, and sink had all arrived and were waiting in the garage to be installed.

Lucas was growing impatient and asked Sybil, "What's going on? The workers haven't been here in a week."

"I know the office manager, Gail," she replied. "I'll give her a call."

She knew Gail because their daughters had attended the same elementary school, so she expected an easy conversation. Sybil called the next morning. "Good morning, Gail. Can I speak to Lenny?"

"Hi Sybil. Lenny has been reassigned to other jobs," the office manager answered curtly.

"Since when? This is the first I'm hearing of it," Sybil answered in disbelief. "Why didn't Harry discuss this with us?"

"We're short on project managers, but we have assigned you a new foreman, Gino. He will get in touch with you." Before Sybil could reply, Gail said goodbye and hung up.

Later in the day, a short, stocky man about thirty years of age with dark hair and muscular forearms paid them a visit.

"Hi, my name is Gino and I take over for Lenny," he said with a thick Italian accent.

"Are you a project manager?" inquired Lucas.

"No, but I work for Harry for five years and I fix your house."

"Have you supervised jobs like this before?" said Sybil.

"I am doing three now. How can I help you?"

"There is no one working on the house," answered Lucas.

"We are waiting for the plumber to fix a pipe in the bathroom," Gino explained.

Sybil crossed her arms. "We've been waiting for a week. Where is he?"

"He's busy with a big job in Bellmore," replied Gino, "but he be here in a few days."

Lucas was losing his patience. "What about the rest of the house? Can't you start working on another room?"

Gino looked annoyed and walked around looking at each room. "I talk to the carpenter; he can start building your room." He pointed to Lucas's study.

"Okay, when will he start?"

"He's working on other jobs, but he has a few days before next one and can do it now."

<hr />

The next day a carpenter came and began rebuilding his office. He worked on the molding, then the mantle of the fireplace, and started working on building bookshelves.

After two days he stopped coming. Lucas and Sybil always hosted Christmas dinner, and the holidays were rapidly approaching. They were hoping that most of the work would be done, but not at this snail's pace. Lucas was fuming. He decided to follow up with a phone call to the new foreman.

"Hello Gino," said Lucas in a bellicose tone of voice. "The carpenter disappeared, and the plumber still hasn't come. You're in charge. What's going on?"

"They're on other jobs but finish soon."

Lucas took a deep breath before answering. "Lenny said the

project would be finished in January. How is that going to happen if no one is working on it?"

"I have workers who can do floor tiles," answered Gino.

"The floor tiles are supposed to be done last so they don't get scratched by all the workers bringing in materials," explained Lucas. "As the project head you should know that."

"Okay, we wait on the tiles. I'll check to see when the electrician and carpenter can come."

"Not the electrician. The plumber," Lucas corrected him. "He needs to fix the pipe in the bathroom."

Lucas felt stymied. Sybil wanted another foreman, but each time she called the office, Gail made excuses and Harry never returned her calls. Not sure what to do, Lucas called Peter for advice.

"I'm having all kinds of difficulty with my contractor," he said when Peter answered. "The workers start on one room and take off, never completing what they started. We tried reaching Harry to complain, but he's not around either."

"My daughter is using a different contractor, but she's having similar problems with her house," Peter replied. "The contractors have taken on more jobs than they can handle. Sandy has been like a jackpot for them. FEMA has distributed so much money to homeowners that they want to cash in by taking as many jobs as possible. That's why they don't have enough plumbers, electricians, kitchen designers, and laborers to go around. But what leverage do you have? If you fire him, your renovations will be delayed even further. A new contractor will have the same difficulty getting workers."

Lucas knew that Peter was right. We're all in the same boat, he thought. It made no sense starting with someone new, especially since he had already paid half the cost of the project. January came and went, and the renovations were far from complete.

While waiting to get the project back on track, Lucas received a check from the National Flood insurance program for $49,000. That wasn't the amount that the FEMA inspector had told him. He still had his telephone number and called him. He tried not to sound too aggressive.

"Hello, Mr. Holly. You visited my home in Massapequa a week after the storm. Your report appraised the damage at $61,000, but the check I just received is for twelve thousand less."

"Yes, I remember the house," said Mr. Holly. "Let me check your file and see what happened." Half an hour later, he called back, "I have your file in front of me, and my estimate was for $61,000. It appears that there was a second engineering report requested by the insurance company. My report was overridden."

"That can't be," insisted Lucas. "No one else came in here to do a damage assessment."

"They don't have to. Some insurance companies hire engineering firms to do second appraisals to reduce their liability. It looks like they have reviewed my notes and pictures and have come up with different interpretations."

"You mean they disagree with your findings?"

"Yes, they may attribute some of the damage to a pre-existing problem due to aging or defect in the house, rather than damage caused by the storm. I would advise that you hire an independent engineer to do a third appraisal. If his estimate is close to mine, FEMA will award you the money you rightfully deserve. Have you begun repairs?"

"Yes, the walls have been fixed," Lucas replied.

"Then show them the pictures you took the day after the storm and the copy of the report I left you."

Lucas followed his suggestions. The third engineering report validated the claims made by the original, so he forwarded it with an appeal letter to FEMA. It would be another four months of deliberation before the appeal was settled so he could receive a second check from the National Flood Insurance program for $12,000. Fortunately, Lucas got the right advice and had the means to appeal the award. He wondered how many people who didn't have the resources got cheated. For years following Sandy, Lucas read stories in newspapers about how insurance companies and engineering firms were sued by victims, revealing many cases of fraud.

Lucas was particularly incensed with another kind of exploitation he witnessed. He thought of his friend Barry who was fighting to keep his home. Builders bought out homeowners who did not have the money to fix their homes. Many were older homeowners like Barry who were living on fixed incomes. In the dawn of a new year, 2013, he was astonished to see vacant lots springing up throughout the south shore. Builders bought damaged properties and leveled the house with the intention of building a larger one for a huge profit.

All they care about is money, he thought to himself. Do they ever stop to consider the damage they are doing to people? To the community that they grew up in. Many of these people were their neighbors, for Christ's sake. They may have gone to school with their sons and daughters. In their childhood, many of these profiteers played in the soccer, baseball, and basketball leagues. They may have been coached by these elderly residents and benefited from their mentorship. Despite the many acts of kindness he witnessed and experienced after Sandy, it pained Lucas to see the exploitation of people he knew by their fellow Massapequans.

CHAPTER 19

# THE POLITICS OF DISASTER RELIEF AID

I t was late December. Sybil went to the bank to extend her credit line limit so she could pay the mounting bills. While waiting for a bank official, she saw Barry meeting with a manager, his face red. With hands flailing and desperation in his voice, he was trying to persuade the stoic and seemingly indifferent supervisor. Her neighbor was obviously in distress, so she decided to wait for him. As he got up to leave the bank, she approached him.

"Hi Barry. I know that it's none of my business, but you seem very agitated. Is everything okay?"

"No, things are awful." He was out of breath and exhausted. "I applied for a reverse mortgage and was turned down because of the condition of my home. They wanted me to repair the house before approving it, but I don't have the funds. I can make repairs once I get the money, but that's not how it works. I came here today to appeal the decision, and I got nowhere. That guy could care less; he just blew me off."

"So sorry to hear that," she said. "What a terrible time of year to go through this!"

"I'm certainly not in the holiday spirit. It was my last chance of keeping my house." His voice quivered. "I have been through a lot in my life, Sybil. I grew up poor and had to work two jobs in high school to help my father support the family. I managed to start a successful business, bought a house, put both my kids through college, and even survived bankruptcy five years ago when my business went under. But I'm a survivor and found a way to make things work until now."

"I wish I had financial advice to give you, but it's not my field," Sybil said meekly. "But I know friends who have sought help from our congressman, Mr. Peterman. He has assisted them with financial and legal problems. Do you know him?"

"Actually, I do. I attended a Chamber of Commerce meeting several years ago where he was the guest speaker. My business was in trouble, and after the meeting I spoke to him seeking advice. He referred me to some government agencies that explained bankruptcy procedures and how to best protect myself."

"You have nothing to lose. Why don't you make an appointment to see him?"

"You're right," Barry perked up. "He helped me once before. Maybe he can again. I'm so glad I ran into you. Thanks for the suggestion."

<hr>

Barry made an appointment to see Congressman Peterman, who was inundated with constituent problems but made time to see him. He prepared for the meeting by bringing all of the damage estimates from contractors, and letters from FEMA and from the bank that declined his reverse mortgage. He dressed up for the meeting. In his generation, making the right impression by wearing appropriate attire was important.

He waited in the reception area for about twenty minutes. His legs were shaking. The congressman walked out of his office and approached Barry.

"Sorry to keep you waiting," greeted the congressman. "We have so many needy people in the aftermath of the storm."

"I know," Barry replied. "I am one of them."

"Please come into my office so we can discuss your situation."

As they sat down, Barry explained his circumstances and the hopelessness he felt.

"I came to you because you helped me once before when I was contemplating filing bankruptcy on my business."

"Yes," replied Congressman Peterman as he stood from his desk to get water for Barry from the cooler in the corner of the room. "I remember you had a family-run hardware store that went under because the big home improvement chains like Home Depot and Lowe's took over your customer base."

"You referred me to some government agencies that helped me get through it," replied Barry. "I'm trying to stay in my house, but I don't have the funds to fix it, and I can't get FEMA and banks to help me."

"Your best bet is the federal government," answered Peterman. "President Obama has calculated that a bill of $60B was needed for disaster relief. Some of that money would be allocated to help homeowners in your situation."

"When will that money be available?" asked Barry.

"That's the problem," responded the congressman. "In the past these bills would pass through the Congress quickly. There was no partisanship because public officials all recognize that it was their duty to help with constituents in need regardless of where they lived. However, since the Republicans took the house in 2010, that has changed. Many new congressmen were part of the Tea Party movement, which believes in reducing government spending and lowering the budget deficit. They claimed that much of the bill was "pork spending" that wasn't related to assisting homeowners and businesses. Democrats disagreed. They defended those appropriations as related to protecting people against future storms. In other words, fortifying the coast against extreme weather events and improving weather forecasting."

"I heard there was a bill in Congress, but it wasn't passed," said Barry.

"Actually, it passed the Senate, but it was not taken up by the house. Speaker Boehner yielded to pressure from his conservative right wing who demanded that there must be budget cuts from other areas to pay for the bill. He didn't bring up the bill for a vote. My congressional colleagues from Long Island and New Jersey and I confronted him on it, but he just let the bill die."

"Is that the last of it? What's going to happen now?"

"It will have to be introduced in the new Congress, but that means a big delay. Furthermore, it has now become a partisan issue because the congressmen who oppose are right-wing conservatives from southern and western states who were not affected by the storm. On the other hand, the people most affected are from liberal blue states. It has become not only a regional divide but an ideological one."

"Where does that leave people like me?" asked Barry.

"I am very confident that some disaster relief bill will be passed in the next Congress, and it will be given top priority," replied the congressman. "My advice to you is hold on. Borrow money from friends and relatives if you have to because help will be coming."

Barry slumped into the chair and said, "Easier said than done. I'm not sure that I can hang on that long, and there are no guarantees."

<hr />

When she heard Barry's story, Sybil was tearful. "I'm sorry that happened to you," she said over the phone. "Lucas and I have had our share of financial troubles, and it hurts to hear of yet another person going through trials like this."

"I don't know what to do about it," Barry told her. "I hate having to wait on my government or my bank to come through."

But in time Barry had bittersweet news to share with Sybil. Two disaster relief bills were finally passed on the last day of January, 2013. But by then, Barry had decided to sell to a builder who gave him a cash offer for $200,000 less than what the house was worth before Sandy.

"My heart sank on the day I signed over the house," he told Sybil later. "It's just that the rug got pulled out from under me. I couldn't afford to keep it."

Sybil felt helpless to offer anything but a condolence. "Lucas and I are so sad to hear the news," she said. "A lot of people are facing the same reality. All I can say is that you guys are survivors and will find a new life."

"Yeah," he said, his voice shaking. "Surviving is costly, but you're right. I need to move on from this."

# CHAPTER 20

# THE LONG BEACH BOARDWALK

The legislation that was passed by Congress consisted of two bills totaling $60B, and almost $10B went to FEMA to help homeowners rebuild. Most of the balance went to communities whose devastated infrastructure needed repairs. A community project that needed to be addressed was the Long Beach boardwalk. Sandy had destroyed many of the boardwalks along the Jersey Shore, Staten Island, Brooklyn, Queens, and Long Island. The epicenter of the storm surge in Nassau County occurred at Long Beach where over ten feet of water came from the ocean and bay to inundate most of the city of thirty thousand. Waters from the ocean and bay met in many sections of the city. The one-hundred-year-old boardwalk was pummeled by waves that shattered the boards and benches. Several sections of the boardwalk collapsed, and parts of it drifted out to sea while other remains floated inland and were deposited on the streets.

The boardwalk was an iconic symbol of the city. Residents from all over Long Island and Queens flocked to it on summer days. While visitors outside Long Beach had to pay a fee to use the beach, the boardwalk was free to everyone. It was used extensively by walkers, runners, bikers, and people of all different ages. There were many fundraisers, political rallies, and cultural events that were hosted on its deck. It was in many ways the heart of the community. The restoration of the boardwalk became not only important to Long Beach, but it became a symbol of resiliency for Long Island.

Lucas had been a frequent visitor to the boardwalk. It was a favorite destination of his bike club. He read in Newsday that there would be a farewell ceremony on January fifth that was open to all. Since Peter was a member of the bike club, Lucas decided to call to see if he would be interested in going. Peter agreed to join him, and that morning they drove to Long Beach.

As they approached the oceanfront, Lucas commented, "So many homes are still damaged with missing walls and open roofs. The Allegra Hotel's windows and doors were smashed and is still closed."

"At least they cleaned up the sand," said Peter. "There were piles of sand all over the city, some several feet high. So much sand got into the drainage system that sewers and toilets still don't work right."

They pulled up to Grand Boulevard where over a thousand people were assembling.

"It's amazing to see how much the boardwalk meant to these people," said Lucas.

"It's been around for so long," replied Peter. "My grandfather often told us stories of coming here as a teenager."

Once everyone was seated, state politicians and city council members spoke about the importance of the boardwalk to the Long Beach community. It was an economic lifeline for the city as it drew people from all over the island. They tried to use its reconstruction as a rallying point to uplift a demoralized community. City Manager Jack Schnirman shouted, "Today is the beginning of the real comeback, and we say goodbye to an old friend but promise to get ready to rebuild bigger, stronger, better, and safer."

The audience then listened to a historian reminisce about all the celebrities that had performed on its deck. Names from the distant past such as Fred Astaire, Charlie Chaplin, and Rudolph Valentino had all entertained there. Its rich history included many summer concerts, and more recently the annual polar bear splashes.

Some long-time residents spoke movingly about heartfelt memories from their formative years. An elderly widow told a story about how her husband had proposed marriage to her on a moonlit evening on the boardwalk seventy years ago. Some younger residents spoke about sneaking out at night during their teen years to meet friends under the boardwalk where they listened to music and drank beer.

One man who grew up in Long Beach came from California to attend the event. He read a short story he had written from the perspective of the boardwalk, relating all the happy moments and wonderful events that it had shared with the city residents for nearly one hundred years. The story ended with the boardwalk thanking the people and wishing them good luck with rebuilding their community. Lucas looked around and saw how many people were brought to tears by the story.

At the end of the ceremony, the city manager invited the audience to a roped-off section of the boardwalk to take a piece of it as a remembrance. Lucas and Peter followed the many who accepted the invitation.

They picked up a few broken boards and began debating which to keep. Suddenly, Lucas dropped them and looked at Peter. "I can't do this. It doesn't seem right to me."

"Why not?" a puzzled Peter replied.

"Before power was restored, I was leery about leaving my house at night unattended. I saw so many warning signs for looters. Taking a piece of the boardwalk almost feels like looting."

"But the event organizers invited you to take a part of it."

"Yes, but you heard the stories that people told." Lucas, choked with emotion, walked away from the remains of the shattered deck.

"It had so much meaning to them that I feel like an intruder. They should take a piece because it was an important part of their personal history, but for me it would only be a souvenir that I will put in my basement and never look at again. I feel like a grave robber."

"I see your point," Peter dropped the splintered boards.

For the next several weeks, a demolition company removed the remains of the boardwalk so construction of the new one could begin.

---

It was mid-August, and Lucas's bike group was meeting in East Rockaway. Dean, a retired earth science teacher, was leading the ride to the new Long Beach boardwalk. He was an environmentalist who had led many rides to the old boardwalk and had closely followed the reconstruction of the new one. As they unloaded the bikes from their cars, Dean spoke to them.

"I learned last week that about 90 percent of the boardwalk is complete, and they're opening the finished sections to the public."

"I heard that the wood for the planks was imported from Brazil. A tropical hardwood with a life span of fifty years," replied Lucas.

"What did it cost them to build it?" inquired Sybil.

"It will cost $44M by the time it's complete," answered Peter.

Lucas raised an eyebrow. "I would imagine their taxes are going up."

"Probably not," speculated Dean, "since they didn't pay for it. FEMA is covering 90 percent of the cost and the state is picking up the rest."

They encountered heavy traffic and many red lights getting to Long Beach but riding on the new boardwalk made it worthwhile. The deck was incredibly smooth and a rich deep brown color.

The lights and handrails had a charming antique quality. They rode for almost two miles as the last section of about a quarter of a mile was still under construction. They had lunch at their favorite bagel shop off the boardwalk.

As they sat at an outdoor table enjoying lox, eggs, and cream cheese on their bagel sandwiches, Sybil marveled. "To build this beautiful structure in about six months is quite an accomplishment."

"You're right," replied Dean. "Sometimes it takes a tragedy to bring out the best in us. The people wanted their boardwalk back, and the people made it happen."

Dean's benediction was as tasty as their lunch. It seemed surreal as they gazed over the ocean that this same body of water which had pummeled and destroyed the community was now a welcome neighbor in the reconstructed city.

# CHAPTER 21

# THE PSYCHOLOGICAL IMPACT

L ucas was panting, sweaty, and exhilarated. He had just finished biking to Jones Beach via the bike path from Cedar Creek Park. This was a favorite route of the bike clubs he belonged to. He parked his bike on the boardwalk and was eating an orange while sitting on one of the benches that face the ocean. It was a beautiful sunny day with blue skies and temperatures in the upper sixties. The bench was shadowed by a wooden overhang, and with the ocean breeze in the dry air, he was chilly. He decided to walk on the beach toward the surf where it was sunny and warmer. The closer he walked to the shore, the louder the soothing sound of waves breaking on the beach grew. It was so relaxing that he decided to sit on the sand and take in the rhythmic sounds of nature.

He lay down and closed his eyes to absorb the tranquility around him. Suddenly, the gentle sounds of the wave action were interrupted by a loud roar. Lucas opened his eyes and a huge wave about twelve feet high crested about twenty feet in front of him, heading right at him. He determined immediately that he could not outrun it, so he had to brace for the impact. What position would best protect him from the vicious blow he was about to receive? He decided to curl up into a ball; he would meet his fate in the fetal position. The roar grew louder as the monster wave was only seconds away. Lucas closed his eyes and held his breathe in terror. "Oh my God," he screamed. Suddenly, he felt two arms around his body cradling him in his bed.

"Lucas, wake up; you're having a nightmare again," pleaded Sybil.

"That was terrifying," he said in a cold sweat.

"What was terrifying?"

He trembled. "I was at Jones Beach, and a tremendous wave was about to crash on me."

"You're having these nightmares a lot these days," she responded with a deep sigh. "All related to drowning or being swept away by a storm. I think it's related to that awful night when you were stranded in the middle of the street during Sandy."

He shook his head. "That can't be. Throughout that entire ordeal and the weeks that followed, I never had any nightmares. Why am I just having them now, several months later?"

"I'm not sure," said Sybil. "It reminds me of people who get into fatal car accidents or witness someone getting shot or killed. Those images stay with them for months and even years. I remember after 9/11, counseling services were set up for people who were in the twin towers during the attack or who lost family members. You should call the Red Cross to see if they have anything like that for storm victims."

Lucas did some research and discovered that eight million dollars of disaster relief aid was used to start a program in New York State called Project Hope. It offered crisis counseling for storm victims.

When he told Sybil, she said with conviction, "Lucas, that is what you need!"

Lucas sunk his shoulders. "To tell the truth, it never even crossed my mind. I've always considered myself to be well adjusted and have never needed assistance with personal problems. I've always worked things out on my own."

Sybil put a soft hand on his shoulder. "Lucas, this goes beyond personal problems. The images of that night have impacted you, and the nightmares are a sign that you're having difficulty coping with them. Don't let your male ego get in the way. Everyone needs help at some time or another."

He relented. "You're probably right, Sybil. I have nothing to lose by speaking to someone. I've been experiencing disturbing obsessions about Sandy. I'll go through half a day stressing over the cost of recovery, how we're still having to pick up the pieces. It's even affecting my dreams. I'll call Project Hope tomorrow."

Lucas called the next day and spoke to a counselor who had done extensive work for the American Red Cross in crisis management. He made an appointment to see him. The day of the meeting he was fidgety and arrived early. After a long wait, a young man small in stature who looked like a hippie from the 1960s with long hair and a beard came out to greet him.

"So glad you could make it. My name is Harvey and I'm here to assist you."

"Nice to meet you," replied Lucas. "As I mentioned to you over the phone, I've been having nightmares and trouble sleeping. I'm not sure what's going on, and I'm looking for help."

The counselor nodded with attention. "From what you told me the day you called; it sounds like you have been through a lot."

"Yes, I have. But that's all behind me. We're living in our house while it's being repaired and have returned to a normal routine. This problem would have made sense right after Sandy, but not after all this time."

"Sometimes during a crisis our adrenaline keeps us going," explained Harvey. "But when the crisis is over and the adrenaline is gone, we may start to feel the psychological toll from all the stress. Tell me what is keeping you up at night."

"I have a hard time going to sleep, and when I do I often wake up in fear."

"Tell me about your nightmares."

"Okay." He took a deep breath. "I'm not used to talking about them. You might think it's strange, but I get jittery and feel my blood pressure rise when talking about the nightmares. The last one was terrifying. A huge wave was about to crash over me, and I woke up screaming. I was sweating and shaking."

"Do you ever experience this kind of fear when you're awake?"

Lucas, feeling anxious, stared at a painting of a sunset on the wall to calm himself. "On several occasions when I was home alone at night, I started to feel nervous and would look outside at the street."

"Harvey leaned in a bit, looking directly into his eyes. "What were you looking for?"

"Not sure. Once I fell asleep watching TV and thought I heard the sound of water going down the stairs to my basement."

"Is that what happened the night of the flood?" asked the counselor.

"Yes, it was so shocking," replied Lucas. He went on to explain to the counselor the terror he experienced being stranded in the street alone at night, during the height of the storm, while his car filled up with water. How the three of them battled to keep the water out of the house and how defeated they felt when they had to abandon the lower two levels. Finally, the feeling of helplessness they experienced as the water surrounded and submerged their property.

"It sounds like you were traumatized," Harvey observed.

"I'm exhausted just talking about it," said Lucas. "The tension from that night just seems to rise to the surface. It was traumatic, but why am I feeling the fear five months later?"

"Perhaps you suppressed what happened that night," Harvey speculated. "It was too scary to think about, so you shut these terrifying images out of your mind, and they are now coming back.

Revisit that evening and allow yourself to feel the fear. Talk about the event so you can provide an outlet for your feelings."

"I see your point," replied Lucas. "The nightmare about the wave is really the fear I experienced that night that is coming out in a different form. By giving that fear an outlet, the nightmares may disappear."

"That's right. Let it come to the surface so you can confront it."

Lucas found the counseling helpful because he connected his nightmares to the fear he repressed the evening of the storm. But he still had so much unfinished business regarding the storm which prompted him to make another appointment the following week.

At their next meeting, Lucas began by reporting that he had tried some of Harvey's suggestions. "I spoke to my wife and daughter about their reactions to that awful night. Sybil said she experienced anxiety, including flashbacks for the next several days, which did make it difficult to sleep, but now she feels much better."

"It sounds like the trauma affected her differently," commented Harvey. "What about your daughter?"

"Gina said that the first few days she was focused on helping us. She and her friends were invaluable in moving all our flooded belongings to the curb. But her first day back to college, she broke down and cried. I guess she had some adrenaline going as well, but the trauma caught up to her. She's fine now, but when I brought her home for Thanksgiving, I noticed that seeing the house stripped down to its studs really affected her. It must have brought back those painful memories."

"Each of you lived through the same event but reacted to the trauma differently," observed Harvey. "Did you revisit that evening with them and allow yourself to relive the fear?"

"Yes, but only for several minutes," replied Lucas. "It got too intense, and I knew it upset my wife."

"That's understandable. Have you been able to sleep better?"

"I still wake up at night, but now I'm starting to have flashbacks so I can remember what produced the fear." He paused. "I have another concern that I would like to discuss with you."

"Sure, what's that?" asked Harvey.

"I have an obsession with Sandy. Whenever I speak to people who live south of Merrick Road, I ask if their home was flooded. If it was, I need to hear all the details. Just last week the woman who cuts my hair told me that water was shooting out of the sewer on her block during the storm surge, and that her neighbor's hot tub wound up on the front lawn. I must have asked her a million questions."

Harvey leaned in with interest. "Do the stories make you feel better?"

"No better or worse. It's like I have a craving to hear the stories. I become even more obsessed if their experience was like mine. I met a school board member in the grocery store whose elderly uncle lives across the street from her. That night she had to walk through three feet of water to check on him. This triggered my obsession. 'What kind of debris was in the water? I almost stepped on a dead animal, what about you?' I became fixated on every word of her story and could envision it happening as if I were there."

"Do you become fixated only in their stories, or are there other examples you can give me of this obsession?"

"When I heard about how the beaches were pounded by the surf, Gina and I took a ride to Field Six of Jones Beach. The concession was protected by a thick glass door which was cracked in several places. I imagined how powerful the waves were that cracked that glass. Parts of the eastbound lane of Ocean Parkway was uplifted by the storm surge and washed away. We drove on the westbound lane to observe the damage. I wondered how the water could have dug up the road like that."

The counselor hummed to himself. He had something to share.

"When I was in Haiti after the earthquake, I heard people express similar fascination with the damage done to buildings, bridges, and roads. Maybe during these catastrophic events, the mind just needs to process the reality of what happened. People often feel a loss of control during these times. You reported feeling helpless that night as your house filled with water. Perhaps reviewing all these facets of Sandy helps you regain that sense of control that was lost that evening."

Lucas considered the implication. "Is this something that will pass with time?"

"Most likely," said Harvey. "But if you would like I can refer you to a therapist who specializes in trauma."

Lucas gave it some thought. "I think I'm going to wait. These two meetings have given me a lot to think about, but if I continue having difficulty sleeping or still experiencing this obsession a year from now, I will go to therapy. Thanks for your help. Your explanations have made me feel better."

Shortly after his meeting with Harvey, Lucas's sleep disturbance did improve, but his obsession with the storm continued. In the spring, when he rode with his bike group to Heckscher State Park and the adjoining communities of Great River and Oakdale, he looked for signs of destruction caused by Sandy. Whether it was shrubs or tress that were uprooted or killed by the saltwater, or homes that were in disrepair, he stopped to observe and asked questions of residents. That summer he went to his favorite ocean resort in Montauk, the Royal Atlantic. Lucas spoke to John, one of the owners, about Sandy. While in his office, John showed him pictures of the flood that reached the seven-story tower in the center of town, which is half a mile from the shore.

Looking at the picture, his eyes widened in awe. "You must have been terrified. This place must have felt like an island in the sea, just like I felt in my house."

"Yes, I was," replied John. "I have been here over forty years and have never seen anything like it. The waves were huge. They wiped out all the sand dunes in front of the hotel, exposed the foundation, and flooded our basement."

John showed Lucas another picture of the foundation of the Royal Atlantic completely exposed by the waves. "My God, the foundation looks like a huge cement block holding the hotel high in the air. Did the waves reach the hotel rooms?" Lucas asked, trying to imagine the ferocity of the storm.

"No. We were in the office that evening and could feel the vibrations of the waves crashing into the foundation. The biggest waves got close but never reached the first-floor rooms. The hotel is twenty feet above the beach, so you can imagine how big the waves were."

Lucas was shivering just thinking about the monster waves. "Jesus, you were that close to losing everything."

Stories like that fed his obsession about Sandy for months. Lucas vicariously experienced people's shock and the threat they felt as Mother Nature devoured their world. The more stories he heard about their fears, the less he was preoccupied about his own. People's reactions were like his and helped normalize the fear he felt that night. With time and many stories later, his obsession was gradually fading away. The nightmares occurred less often and eventually disappeared. There were days when he could look out at the ocean without fear.

# CHAPTER 22

# NEW YORK RISING

In the early months of 2013, Barry's house became an eyesore. It had been abandoned for three months and was starting to look like a haunted house without the ghosts. Sybil decided to call him.

"We really miss you and Barbara," she said to him. "I feel terrible that I never said goodbye."

"I have to apologize," he said with sorrow. "We thought of coming back after we sold the house to say farewell to all of our neighbors, but it was too painful."

"Where are you living now?"

"We're staying in a one-bedroom apartment in Westchester County a few miles from my son. We're hoping to find a small condo in a development, but finances are tight right now. The guy who bought our house got a real bargain. I sold him the house at $200,000 less than I would have gotten for it before Sandy."

"Well, not only did he take advantage of you," she lamented, "but he's making it tough on all of us. The house has been abandoned for so long that several of the windows have cracked glass, and he boarded them up. The vegetation is overgrown, and several shingles from the siding are falling off. Stray cats are making a home in the backyard and have become a nuisance to the other families on the block."

"So sorry to hear that," said Barry.

"Do you know what his plans are?"

"All I know is that he wasn't planning to live there. He bought it for investment purposes."

"Do you know how I can get in touch with him?" said Sybil. "I want to know what his intentions are."

"I know he will be at the house one day next week," replied Barry. "I left some of my things in the garage, and he's going to let me in. I'll call you and let you know what day and time he'll be there."

"Thanks, I'd appreciate that."

In the following days, she and Lucas prepared a list of questions for the new owner. Lucas consulted with the town to see what the rights of homeowners were when a neighbor's home was abandoned and became dilapidated. He was encouraged to hear that the new owner could be fined for not maintaining the property, so they did have some leverage. Barry called a few days later. The builder was coming at the end of the week, so Sybil planned on meeting him at the front of his house. Friday morning a man in a pickup truck pulled into the driveway of the abandoned home. She was there to greet him.

"Excuse me, are you the owner of this house?"

The thin man about forty dressed in denim overalls with a construction hat turned around to her and said, "Yes, my name is Rudy. Can I help you ?"

"My husband and I live next door. We as well as many others on the block are upset over the condition of the house," complained Sybil. "It's ugly to look at and brings down the value of our homes."

"I have to apologize," Rudy said, nodding his head in agreement. "There are over a dozen homes I'm working on, but I'll be getting to this one soon. In fact, it will be leveled before the end of the month."

"Why not just fix it?" she asked.

"That wouldn't be very profitable for me. To make money on

this, I need to build a much larger home and then flip it for a nice profit," he explained. "Many of the local builders are doing the same thing. There are hundreds of homes on the South Shore like this one."

He had piqued her curiosity. "So, what is this house going to look like?"

"I'm building a contemporary four-bedroom colonial that has lots of windows and closets with a double car garage," answered Rudy. "That's the design that young couples want today."

"It's going to look like a misfit," replied Sybil. "All the homes on the block are either split level or high ranch. It runs counter to the character of the block, and the house will be oversized for the lot it is on. I think it will turn off young buyers."

Rudy shook his head. "Splits and high ranches are outdated. This block was built in the 1950s, and these homes were designed for the post-World War II generation. Closets are too small, the garages are for only one car, and the kitchens are antiquated. They didn't have dishwashers and microwave ovens back then. Because of Sandy the character of many blocks will change. There's going to be a lot of new building on the South Shore. Almost every block will have new or reconstructed homes, which is a good thing. It will raise the value of your home."

"Well, I hope you're right. If that means young families moving in, we're all for that."

⋘≫◆⋙≪

By late fall the house was completed. It did look like an anomaly, but it was beautiful. The house was worth $300,000 more than any other home and raised the value of all the other homes as Rudy had predicted. Many young families came to look at it. The wife of one couple was particularly interested. Hannah grew up right across the street and had many great childhood memories of living on

West End Avenue. Her mother still lived there, another reason she wanted it. Hannah and her husband Ed were in their late twenties, and it was a great house for a couple looking to start a family. Lucas and Sybil were thrilled when they bought the house. Being the same age as this young couple when they bought their home, they saw so much of themselves in this young couple.

But something went wrong; rumor had it that the closing was delayed. Lucas was concerned and decided to call Ed and ask him about the closing date.

"We have a major problem," replied Ed in a solemn voice. "The bank requires flood insurance and when we applied, FEMA turned us down. They said that we're in a flood zone and because of the extensive damage the house sustained during the Sandy, it has to be elevated."

"Well, our house is in the same flood zone, and we suffered extensive damage from the storm as well," replied Lucas. "Why weren't we required to elevate to keep our flood insurance?"

"It has to do with the cost of repairs. To tear down the house and rebuild it, the cost exceeded 50 percent of the market value of the house pre-Sandy," explained Ed. "So to qualify for insurance we have to elevate the house."

"That explains it," said Lucas. "Our repairs never reached that level. What are you going to do?"

"I'm looking to see if there are banks who don't require flood insurance. To elevate the house, it would cost us $130,000, and we can't afford it."

"I doubt you'll find that bank, especially after Sandy," replied Lucas. A thought came to him. He had heard about Governor Cuomo launching the New York Rising Recovery program to provide financial assistance to homeowners whose houses were damaged during hurricanes Irene, Lee, and Sandy. He shared with

Ed how, as part of the relief aid package passed, the Housing and Urban Development department has received several billion dollars and was funding the program. Homes that required elevation were also included. If the young couple was accepted, the NYR program would pay the cost. Ed thanked him and decided to investigate it.

The young couple spoke to the program administrators the next day and were encouraged to apply. The claim process was arduous and required extensive paperwork. Some of the documentation was difficult to get from Barry since he was now living in Westchester. The funds were being tightly monitored because of the abuse of the system that occurred after Hurricane Katrina; people took advantage of loose oversight. Applicants had to meet the guidelines of both HUD and New York Rising. After two months of processing, they were finally approved. The closing on their house was delayed for several months, but Rudy was willing to wait. It would be difficult to sell the house to potential buyers if they couldn't get flood insurance. Ed and Hannah lived in her mother's house across the street while their home was elevated.

Sybil and Lucas watched the construction job with awe as it took place in stages. The project began with workers sliding large steel beams under the house, and with specialized hydraulic jacks, they lifted the house nine feet above its foundation. It was held in that position for the next several weeks. The workers used cement and wood pilings to build up the foundation. When they were finished, the house was lowered onto its new base. After wiring, plumbing, and gas lines were reconnected, they patched up the empty spaces, and the house and foundation became one structure again. After each stage was completed, an inspector from New York Rising certified the work, and the contractor was paid for that part of the job. The end result was that the house was now seven feet higher than before. Instead of having five stairs leading to the front door, there were now fourteen. Ed and Hannah finally were able to obtain flood insurance and closed on the home in the spring of 2014.

On one of their evening walks, Sybil commented to Lucas, "Massapequa sure has a different look. It seems like almost every block has new huge or elevated homes like the one next door to us. They tower over the neighboring homes and look so out of place."

"The blocks with waterfront properties look even stranger. They're full of elevated homes now, we'll have to get used to it. It's the new normal."

"It's almost comical watching people going up all those stairs with bags from shopping," said Sybil.

Lucas smirked. "Yes, some look like they need oxygen when they get to the fourteenth step."

Sybil laughed. "I guess it is one of Sandy's legacies."

He agreed with her. The storm had taken well-maintained, uniform suburban communities and transformed them into a patchwork of tall and low homes with disjointed architectural designs. A strange combination of disaster and opportunity.

"Strange appearance aside," said Lucas, "so many people were saved by New York Rising. I know people have complained about all the paperwork, delays, and excessive regulations, but without their help, those people would never have been able to elevate or rebuild their homes. Critics often point out that our taxes are too high, and the government takes too long to get things done, but they really came through this time for the storm victims."

Sybil concurred.

# CHAPTER 23

# THE FIRST ANNIVERSARY

As late October of 2013 approached, Lucas started to plan for Sybil's birthday dinner. They had invited the whole family—their children, her parents, and her sisters.

Sybil set plates and glasses on the table for dinner. "I can't believe another year has passed."

"And what a year it has been," replied Lucas. "It's hard to believe all that we've been through since Sandy."

"I'm glad everyone can come," said Sybil. "I want to celebrate how helpful they were to us this year. Kathy, Debbie, and their husbands. We were practically homeless when they offered to help."

"Dick and Sharon were helpful too," agreed Lucas. "By lending us their car, your parents made it possible for us to move forward in our recovery efforts."

As the guests arrived the day of her birthday celebration, Lucas and Sybil greeted them warmly. They sat in the living room while Lucas made his new specialty, vegetarian lasagna, in the kitchen. Some wanted to see the work the contractor had done, so Sybil escorted them through the first floor and basement. As they walked down the stairs, Sybil pointed out all the work that was done.

"Wow," said Debbie. "Look at this new floor. And the cabinets above the bar look great."

"The built-in bookcases in Lucas's study are beautiful," added Dick.

"I love the doors that you picked, and the aquamarine color scheme brightens everything. The lower half of your house looks brand new," said Kathy. "You did get something for all your hardship."

Sybil disagreed. "It may look nice, but it wasn't worth it. Living through that horrible night and all the stress that followed was torture. I would never want to go through that again. The contractor ultimately did a good job, but there were so many problems. The project was supposed to be finished in January, but it wasn't completed until June."

"Why so late?" asked Sharon.

"He had so many jobs going on at once and didn't have enough workers. We had an excellent project manager at first, but he was reassigned, and a new inexperienced foreman took over who made plenty of mistakes. I argued with him so often on the phone until the contractor himself got involved and finally finished it."

As they returned to the living room, Sybil thanked them. "Without your help, we would've never gotten through this. Gina, Tara, and Greg helped us clean up the mess. Mom and Dad, lending us your car was a lifesaver while we replaced our cars. Kathy and Todd, you gave us a place to stay, and Debbie and Adam, I appreciate all your support, especially during the first few weeks."

They all acknowledged her gratitude. "By the way, I should get special mention for saving two of the three remaining fish we rescued from Dad's aquarium," Tara said wryly.

Sybil laughed. "Yes, special thanks to you, Tara. They survived all that trauma, and after all the work you did in keeping them alive, they died a few weeks later. I guess they didn't like their new digs."

Everyone was able to share in the laugh.

"Besides the house, is everything back to normal?" asked Debbie.

"In some ways," responded Sybil. "We replaced our three cars; Lucas finally got his after Thanksgiving. He went to the same car dealer where he leased his Ford Edge and got an Escape with no consideration on price for a loyal patron; he paid full price like I did.

But the outside property is still a work in progress. The gardener replaced the shrubs in front of the house, but the yard is still a mess. We had to remove fifteen small trees in the back that died from the salt water. They gave us privacy, so the yard looks bare now. We're going to have to replace them with smaller trees that will take several years to grow in. Likewise, the lawn looked brown this past growing season, and we hope that it will recover by next summer."

"Plants will grow back," Todd remarked. "At least there was no permanent damage."

"Yes, you're right," agreed Sybil. "But I hope I can find peace of mind again. When hurricane season started in June, Lucas and I were constantly checking the weather report. Every time a storm formed in the Caribbean or Gulf of Mexico, we got nervous and were afraid that it was going to turn into a hurricane and come up the East Coast."

"Climate scientists are predicting bigger, stronger, and more frequent hurricanes in the future," said Dick. "Sandy was supposed to be a hundred-year storm, but now a storm like that might come every ten to fifteen years."

"We also don't like this monstrous house being built next door," continued Sybil. "The owners are a lovely young couple, but the house is too big for the property. It's going to look even worse once it's elevated. It is going to dwarf our house."

"Mom, it doesn't sound like you're happy living here," observed Greg.

Sybil paused to reflect on his comment. "I guess we're still trying to adjust to everything that has happened. Sandy has changed our community and instilled a sense of fear. When we first moved here, I didn't even know what a flood zone was. Now when I hear that term, it makes me anxious."

"It's only been a year," Tara said, trying to be reassuring. "Five or six years down the road you may feel more at peace."

"That's true," said Sybil. "But by that time, we may not even be able to afford living here. We spent a lot of money on repairs and have a huge debt that we have to pay off."

"You can repay the debt gradually since your credit line allows you years to repay," Gina chimed in.

"Yes, but we just got a letter from FEMA last week," replied Sybil. It explained that people with food insurance have historically paid a discounted rate. Flood insurance costs a lot more than what homeowners pay. That's why few private insurance companies offer flood coverage. Taxpayers have subsidized some of the cost, but no more. Starting next year, our premium will be going up 9 percent to 17 percent annually."

"Why such a huge range?" asked Todd.

"The letter doesn't explain how they have arrived at those percentages," answered Sybil. "But premiums will increase until homeowners pay the actual cost of flood insurance."

"Does it amount to that much?" asked Sharon.

"Well, when you're paying $3,000 a year, our premium could double in six or seven years," said Sybil. "That will make it more difficult to sell our house when potential buyers are looking at six thousand in flood insurance, in addition to the mortgage, taxes, and the other expenses."

Lucas appeared in the doorway with his cooking apron. "Okay, everyone. Dinner is ready. I think you could all use a break from Sybil's gloom and doom talk."

All the guests took a seat around the dinner table. The aroma of Lucas's marinara sauce delighted his guests. The red wine flowed as they enjoyed the vegetarian lasagna with a serving of the best Italian bread. A salad and side dish of string beans almandine completed a delicious meal.

"I was listening to your conversation from the kitchen," said Lucas. "While Sandy was a terrible experience and a huge financial cost, we were more fortunate than many of our Long Island neighbors. Thousands are still living in trailers, hotel rooms, apartments, or with relatives while their homes are being repaired."

Kathy's jaw dropped in disbelief. "Really? A year later? Shouldn't they be back in their house by now?"

"Many people didn't have insurance, so they had to wait for the federal aid to be passed by Congress. It has taken a long time for that aid to fund New York Rising, the government agency paying for the rebuilding."

"Lucas, I remember sitting around this table a year ago, and we couldn't convince you guys to evacuate," said Dick. "You thought the weather forecasters were hyping it up to increase their viewers."

Lucas nodded slowly. "Yes, I was fooled into thinking that because Gloria and Irene were not a big deal, Sandy wouldn't be either. I'll never underestimate Mother Nature again."

"What would you do differently, Dad?" asked Greg.

"Have you ever seen what they do to prevent the Mississippi River from overflowing in the spring?" asked Lucas.

"They build up the banks of the river with sandbags," answered Dick.

"Exactly. I would pile sandbags four feet high in front of the garage and back door, and then leave."

"You won't stay behind to connect the generator when the power goes out?" said Sybil.

"No," her husband answered emphatically. "I learned the hard way. It's better to be safe than sorry. I would never again jeopardize the safety of my family or me."

"That's good to hear," said Todd. "I never want to share my bathroom with you again."

They all laughed.

After dinner, Gina went to the fridge to take out Sybil's favorite birthday dessert, an ice cream cake. She put candles on it, lit them, and they all sang happy birthday to Sybil. The birthday girl took a long pause before blowing out the candles.

"Wow, Mom," said Tara. "That must have been a very long wish list. Care to share?"

"No, I'm superstitious," replied Sybil. "It may not come true if I share it."

She thought to herself: When I retire, I'm going to sell this house and live in a 55+ community with a club house, swimming pool, organized activities like a Mahjong club and, most importantly, it must be far away from the coast. No more flood zones for me.

# CHAPTER 24

# WHAT THEY LEARNED ABOUT SUPERSTORM SANDY

In November of 2014, there was an exhibition at the American Museum of Natural History in Manhattan called "Nature's Fury." It provided scientific information on the causes of nature's most terrifying events: tornados, earthquakes, volcanic eruptions, and hurricanes. Superstorm Sandy was featured in the hurricanes section. Scientific knowledge about Sandy had accumulated over the two years which better explained its origins, why it became the strongest Atlantic storm in modern times, and why the Eastern Seaboard was vulnerable to the massive damage it caused. Lucas was still obsessed about Sandy and wanted to know the answer to these questions.

Lucas and a few of his friends from the bike club made plans to visit the museum. He was looking forward to it. Speaking with a counselor had helped him resolve unhealthy obsessions and open the door to learning important lessons from the past. On the train ride to the city, Dean often gave tours of the museum to school groups, drawing from his science background. He explained the physics of the storm. Lucas had a basic understanding of how warm ocean water, colliding air masses, and the full moon's gravitational force all combined to create the super storm. But he was still curious about the details.

As they approached the exhibit, they saw a large model of New York Harbor surrounded by Staten Island, lower Manhattan, Brooklyn, and Queens. By pressing a red button, a simulation was set in place showing how the storm gathered strength as it approached the New York City metropolitan area and climaxed with a storm surge that drowned all the waterfront communities bordering the harbor. They were fascinated with the sounds and lights of the automated demonstration.

A bespectacled, scholarly looking man was giving a tour of the exhibit to a group of students who had just arrived. They decided to listen to his presentation. He pointed to a large map with arrows showing the path of Sandy.

"On October 23, Sandy started as a tropical storm in the Caribbean Sea off the coast of Nicaragua. She struck Jamaica as a Category 1 hurricane. As the storm moved north it gathered strength, dumping twenty inches of rain in Haiti and the Dominican Republic. She reached Cuba as an almost Category 3 hurricane, causing extensive damage to the eastern part of the island." Lucas could see that the speaker had his audience hooked. It was so silent you could hear a pin drop.

"As the tempest roared north, she crossed over the Bahamas and stayed a few hundred miles east of Florida. The storm lost some of its power, reverting to a Category 1 hurricane. As she drifted northeast, Sandy pounded the Carolinas with high wind and rain."

His hands were becoming more animated as he continued with Sandy's path northward. "Her transformation into a superstorm occurred when she merged with a cold front from the north, which pushed Sandy closer to the East Coast. She became a post-tropical nor'easter; a combination of hurricane and snowstorm. The storm, fed by the warm water of the Atlantic, became stronger and larger."

The lecturer spread his arms on the map to show the size of Sandy. "At its maximum, Sandy's wind field spanned almost a thousand miles and reached from North Carolina to Maine to the Midwest. Thousands of people in Michigan, which was several hundred miles from the eye, lost all power. It was the largest storm ever recorded in the Atlantic Ocean. In addition to the drenching rain, Sandy dumped up to three feet of snow in West Virginia, Maryland, and western Virginia. Because of its size, a full moon, and the direction of the wind, it created a record storm surge of fourteen feet in New York Harbor that flooded Lower Manhattan and the adjacent areas.

"Sandy made landfall near Atlantic City on the evening of the twenty-ninth and devastated New Jersey and New York, then gradually moved westward and dissipated as she reached Pennsylvania. In her wake, she left two hundred people dead and $60B to $65B of damage. A third of the country, seventeen states felt her effects."

The audience whispered to one another in amazement. Lucas was mesmerized by the tour guide. His explanations put into context what happened that night. There was nothing supernatural about the event. It was just a bunch of freak meteorological factors that combined to produce a cataclysmic event. He thought of being stranded during the storm, feeling surrounded by an evil force seeking to do him harm. There was nothing evil about Sandy, just the work of physics. He felt like a balloon was deflating inside him. The pent-up anxiety he always felt when thinking about her was leaving him and being replaced by an inner calm.

One of the students asked, "Did climate change play any role in her evolution from a mid-size hurricane to a superstorm?"

The tour guide hesitated for a second, gathering his thoughts. "Global warming is not responsible for any single weather event," he answered, "but the properties of the storm and its path were influenced by climate variables. Hurricanes require warm ocean water with typically temperatures of near eighty degrees or higher to fuel them, which explains why so many begin in the Caribbean Sea or Gulf of Mexico. With current warming trends, larger and stronger hurricanes have been more prevalent this century." Turning again to the map, he pointed to the southern states. "For example, let's look at Hurricane Katrina. After she passed through Florida, Katrina gathered tremendous strength here (waving his hand over the Gulf of Mexico) and made its way north to New Orleans in early September of 2005. Higher water temperature also heats up the atmosphere which then enables it to hold greater moisture producing more rain."

He turned to the audience again. "The summer of 2012 was a hot one in the eastern US and Canada. There was a record melting of polar ice in the Arctic. Since the massive snow fields of the Arctic reflects sunlight, they act as a cooling agent. But that summer, because of the record melting, much of the sunlight that ordinarily would be reflected back to the atmosphere was absorbed by the ocean." Students were nodding with understanding. "It is estimated that the water temperature of the Atlantic Ocean where Sandy passed was up to five degrees warmer than normal. In late October, it would be unusual for a hurricane to be able to reach the Northeast; the water wouldn't be warm enough during that time of year to sustain it. Sandy may have never reached New York and New Jersey, but that year the warmer ocean made its path possible."

There was a collective sigh in the audience as if a great mystery had been solved.

"The rising seas also made it more destructive. It is estimated that sea level has risen up to a foot since the early 1900s. Higher sea level gave the surge a higher launching pad, which caused more extensive flooding and larger waves."

Another student raised her hand. "Why did a record-breaking number of people lose power in the city? I've seen pictures of Manhattan in total darkness the night after."

"In most hurricanes, people lose power because the wind causes falling debris to snap power lines," the guide replied. "With Sandy it was mainly flooding that caused the power outages. One of the reasons why so many people lost power is that large buildings near the water, especially the office buildings in Lower Manhattan, often kept their main electrical connections and generators in the basement. When the surge flooded all these buildings, the electrical system and back-up generators were the first to go, leaving these buildings in the dark for days. Since Sandy, city officials have learned their lesson and building codes have been changed. Power stations are now placed on the upper floors where they can't be reached by flooding."

Lucas was so engrossed by the presentation that he had to ask a question that had been nagging him since the storm. "Why didn't natural coastal defenses on Long Island like dunes and barrier beaches better protect waterfront communities?"

"Unfortunately, most of those defenses are gone," replied the lecturer. "In the early part of the twentieth century, Long Island was rural and largely undeveloped. The residents were mainly farmers or bay men who made a living fishing its abundant marine life. That all changed after World War II. As millions of soldiers returned home, married, and started families, there was a great need for housing. Builders like William Levitt developed large communities of affordable housing. To make room for the homes, the land south of Merrick Road and Montauk Highway, which was marsh land, had to be filled in. Wetlands and marshes provide protection against storms; more than half of wave energy is dissipated in the first three meters of marsh vegetation. By 2012, it is estimated that nearly half of the South Shore's wetlands and marshes were gone, which left waterfront communities defenseless to Sandy's on-slaught."

Lucas and his friends looked at each other. "That's true," said Peter. "When my family moved out to Long Island in the late 1940s, it was sparsely populated, mostly farmland."

"I heard they are planning to build a giant sea wall that can be raised during a storm to prevent coastal flooding," said a young woman.

The guide nodded. "Some European countries have had success building sea walls or gates that can prevent storm surges from flooding the coast. As a storm approaches, the gates can be closed to keep out the rising water. Officials in New York City are looking at such concepts to protect lower Manhattan, but it would be very costly."

"That will never work," said Dean. "Environmentalists would be up in arms that we would be altering the ecology of the harbor. Besides, there is no guarantee that it would work with the monster storms of late."

The guide began wrapping up his presentation. "The biggest lesson Sandy taught us is that degrading our natural habitat either through climate change or the overdevelopment of our coast will invite unintended catastrophic consequences. Just when we think that technology has solved the latest problem, Mother Nature reminds us that we can't control her indefinitely. Short-term solutions that provide band-aid approaches to tame nature will undermine the wise, long-term planning needed to live with her in harmony. Our planet has had five periods of mass extinction. The Earth will be here for the sixth, but unless humanity develops a more sustainable philosophy with nature, we may not be." The audience gasped at this notion. Could mankind become extinct?

"Wow, that was a scary way to end his tour," said a pale Lucas, pulling back his collar. "He made it sound like the apocalypse was coming."

"Well, I agree with him," replied Dean. "Look at what they're doing in Long Beach."

"Are you referring to the Superblock?" said Peter.

"Yes," Dean replied. "They are building two huge high-rise condominiums right on the boardwalk instead of protecting the environment."

"That's because of money," said Peter. "More often than not, economic development seems to take precedent over environmental conservation."

"Sad but true," they agreed.

The visit to the museum helped Lucas put the storm into a healthier perspective. He understood the science now, but what about the feeling of being a victim that had been nagging him for two years? Like he was cursed by a sorcerer! But now he saw that there was nothing sinister about it, just bad luck. Being in the wrong place at the wrong time. When you lose ten straight games of blackjack at the casino, you don't conclude that you're a victim of the dealer. It's just bad cards. He compounded bad luck with the poor choices he made during and in the aftermath of Sandy which made things worse. Rather than thinking objectively, he had let his own emotions take over too often during the cyclone and in the weeks that followed. Fortunately, Sybil was there to steady him and provide the logic that often escaped him.

# CHAPTER 25

# THE FIFTH ANNIVERSARY

Much had changed for Lucas and Sybil by the fall of 2017. Gina had graduated from college and was working as a nurse for the NICU of a Long Island Children's hospital. She and her boyfriend, Alex, were living in an apartment in Long Beach. Greg was finishing his MBA at NYU and doing well working for a financial firm in Manhattan. Tara and Jim had married the year before and purchased a home nearby. Earlier that autumn they were blessed with their first child, Jack. Lucas and Sybil were now grandparents and she had retired from teaching, so they had plenty of time to enjoy their grandson.

The four-bedroom Massapequa house had become too big for two people. They were looking for a simpler life where they could travel and spend winters in Florida without worrying about their home during snowstorms and power outages. Sybil and Lucas began looking at condominiums in senior communities. When they found one that was being built in Suffolk County, they began preparing to sell their home. They felt sad about leaving the community where they had raised their children and developed so many friendships over the years. West End Avenue had been the center of their universe for so long, but the threat of more frequent extreme weather events made their decision easier. They just didn't want to live near the water any longer.

Lucas was a long-time member of the Sierra Club and had participated in many hikes and other outdoor activities. Since Sandy he had become an environmental activist participating in rallies that promoted renewable energy. Lucas was a strong believer that climate change was the leading cause of the monster storms, wildfires, droughts, and heat waves that had been occurring more frequently. As someone who had experienced firsthand the fury and destruction of Sandy, he was asked to speak at rallies advocating for renewable energy. Climate scientists presented evidence that burning of fossil fuels was emitting carbon which traps heat in the atmosphere, causing global warming. He had learned from the Sandy exhibit at the museum that warmer ocean temperatures were fueling larger hurricanes. Lucas even spoke at an executive board meeting of LIPA which was considering switching from gas-powered power plants to offshore wind farms to produce electricity. One morning he received an invitation in the mail that piqued his interest.

"Hey Sybil," he called from his study. "They're having an event in Lindenhurst to commemorate the fifth anniversary of Superstorm Sandy."

Curious, she came over to read the letter with him. "Why did they choose Lindenhurst? I thought Nassau County and New York City suffered the greatest damage."

"That's true, but many Suffolk County villages were devastated as well. The Venetian Shores section of Lindenhurst is a low-lying area facing the Great South Bay. It has had a long history of flooding during lunar high tides and storms. If it has flooded during high tides, can you imagine what it went through during Sandy?"

"It must have been twice as bad as it was for us," she speculated.

"Anyway, community organizations such as the Long Island Progressive coalition are hosting the meeting. Want to go with me?"

"It's right before the midterm elections," replied Sybil. "We're going to hear a lot of campaign speeches."

"I know the environmental and community groups hosting it,"

explained Lucas. "And while politicians will be there, they'll keep the focus on how community has fared these past five years."

"Okay, but if I hear too many political speeches, I'm leaving."

They drove to Shore Road Park on a cold, drizzly morning. About two hundred people had gathered for the event. Sybil was right. A state senator and a few assemblymen gathered under a tent near the shoreline, but they didn't speak that day. The speakers were community organizers who fought for the people. They were advocates who lobbied Governor Cuomo, as well as federal and local politicians, to provide more aid to residents who were still struggling.

It was an emotionally charged event with fiery speeches from community representatives. Amidst all the fury, an unassuming middle-aged woman was called to speak to the crowd. As she walked onto the platform, the woman held papers that shook in her hand. As she peered over the crowd, the many lines in her face were evidence that she had been through a lot. Her name was Michele. With a calm and humble demeanor, she told her story.

"Five years ago today, my home, which is three blocks from here, was flooded with several feet of water. During that afternoon, we received orders to evacuate, and I stayed at my sister's house that night. When I returned in the morning, there was a powerboat the size of a small bus on my front lawn. There was so much debris brought in by the storm that it took several minutes to get to my front door. When I got into my house, my entire first floor was unrecognizable. Furniture, pictures, kitchen appliances, decorations, plates, lamps, the television, tables, and broken glass were strewn throughout the rooms. It took a week for my husband, kids, and me to clean up the mess. We had to stay at my sister's house during that time. We filed a claim with FEMA and received an estimate of $110,000 in damages. Our flood insurance was insufficient; it covered only half the amount, and we had to pay the rest. We hired a contractor to do the work and moved back to our property where we lived in a trailer to oversee the reconstruction of our house. After several weeks, the contractor walked away from the job and left the country because of a family problem in Greece.

"We pursued the contractor legally, and it took months to get our money back, but we only recovered a portion of it. By that time, the house had become badly infested with mold. We filed a claim with New York Rising and were accepted into the program. Because of the mold problem and deterioration of the house, an architect from New York Rising determined that the house had to be demolished and rebuilt. We hired a new contractor who removed the entire structure including the foundation. After several months of living in a cramped trailer, we moved to an apartment in the same community. We did receive rental assistance from our Congressman's office.

"The second contractor began rebuilding the house. According to the agreement, he was to get paid by New York Rising in installments. When the payments were not arriving fast enough, he complained, demanding more money from us. He stopped working on our home until we paid him. We didn't have the money to pay him, and New York Rising would not forward any payments in advance. His company eventually walked away from the job. When we complained to New York Rising, they sent an engineer to the site and found that the contractor had put in the wrong foundation for a waterfront home and cracks were appearing in the foundation damaging the first floor. New York Rising declared the case a fraud and pursued the contractor in court. Meanwhile, our half-built house sat there for months. They paid for the foundation that had to be redone but recently notified us that we had reached our limit. They have no more money to give us, and we can't afford to pay for the remaining repairs. We have used up our retirement savings and are broke. Our wonderful neighbors have chipped in by organizing fundraisers, but five years after the storm we are still not back in our house and the end of this nightmare is nowhere in sight."

As Michele neared the end of the story, her voice cracked, and she struggled to maintain her composure. The audience stood in deafening silence while she spoke. The final speaker gave suggestions on what participants could do to help people like Michele, such as calling public officials to demand action.

Lucas and Sybil were stunned to hear of her pain and suffering. They both approached her after the event.

After they introduced themselves, Sybil commented. "We were so moved by your story."

"The way you were treated is despicable," said Lucas, fuming. "These contractors should have been forced to complete their jobs. I can't believe government officials allowed them to get away with it."

"Thanks for your kindness and support," said Michele. "What brought you here today?"

"We also were flooded during Sandy, and it took almost a year to get back to normal," replied Sybil. "But we were able to stay in our home, and while we experienced some of the same frustrations with FEMA and contractors, it's nothing compared to what you have been through."

"How are you and our family coping with all this stress?" said Lucas.

"Not well," she told them, and by the deep lines around her eyes, they couldn't imagine her burden. "My kids are upset because they don't have a normal social life. The apartment is too small to have friends over, and my husband has had to work two jobs to keep up with the bills. I take anxiety medication because I suffer from panic attacks now. Despite all this, we are determined to stay here and fix our home."

"Honestly, I never imagined that there were some people who were still not back in their homes five years later," said Sybil.

"I appreciate that you came today," replied Michele. "Most people don't realize how many displaced people there still are. I belong to a network of victims who still aren't back in their homes. There are at least ten homeowners in this community and probably a couple hundred on Long Island."

"That's outrageous!" said Lucas. "It's so hard to fathom because you never hear of it in the local news."

"The more time has passed, the less attention we receive," added Michele. "You could see that in the audience today. We had only a few local politicians in the audience. No federal officials or members of the governor's office were here. They've forgotten us, and we get little media coverage during these events."

"You make a valid point," answered Sybil. "With the midterm election a week away, you'd think there would be more politicians here today since everyone here will be voting next week."

"There's a reason why they stay away," continued Michele. "No one wants to be associated with a tragedy that happened five years ago and still continues for hundreds of people. It's an embarrassment they'd rather forget. As one Congressman said to me: 'It's time to put this behind you and move on.' He would prefer that we give up our home, sell it to an investor, and move to another community so he doesn't have to look at us and be reminded of his failure. They treat us like lepers and wish we would just go away."

"What a disgrace," seethed Lucas. "They're paid to represent their constituents. There is so much corporate welfare in this country with giant companies that don't pay taxes, and billions in subsidies for the fossil fuel industry. While they can afford to be generous with them, they claim to have no money to help those who need it the most."

Michele nodded. "You're absolutely right. They have the money for people with political clout. We have become a subgroup without a political voice. Someone needs to bring this issue back into the national limelight."

Lucas nodded. "Out of sight, out of mind. I just want you to know that your story will not be forgotten. I speak at Sierra Club events, and I will tell your story. And I'm sure there are people here today who will do the same. By repeating your story over and over, we would be a megaphone that will reach enough people to spur politicians to take action."

"Thank you," said Michele, her eyes filling with tears. "I'm touched by your empathy and willingness to help." She hugged them both.

As they left the park, Lucas heard his wife sniffing. "Are you okay, Sybil?"

"I'm upset and angry," she said. "I came here today thinking that it would be a celebratory occasion. How a devastated community had pulled together and rebuilt itself. Instead, I hear about this poor woman and how she and her family are still suffering five years later. It is so disturbing to me. Listening to her speak, I had flashbacks of that awful night. For me it's in the past, but for her it's still the present."

Lucas leaned over and put his arm around his wife. "You know, one of the principles the Army teaches its soldiers is 'Leave no one behind.' Any casualty of war is never left on the battlefield. Soldiers who are wounded or killed are always brought home. We should do the same. Whether it's telling their story, calling politicians, taking part in fundraisers, or writing to newspapers, we can't leave the storm victims behind. All of us who suffered through Sandy should not rest until everyone is back in their homes."

They got into their car and drove away toward the peaceful horizon. On their way home they passed by many houses, so many of them standing, so many of them fortunate—but not all of them.

There was a group of people who could not put the pain behind them because they were still living it.

# AFTERWORD

As of this writing, the Storm Recovery of the Governor's Office reports that New York Rising accepted 10,261 applications for home repairs or elevation on Long Island. Of these, 363 cases in Nassau County and 130 in Suffolk County are still not completed. While many people have moved back into their homes and are waiting for final inspection, some are still not back in their homes eight years later. Michele is one of them.

# ABOUT THE AUTHOR

**Luciano Sabatini** is an adjunct professor at Hofstra University where he teaches graduate courses in bereavement and group counseling to students in mental health programs. He also serves as the bereavement coordinator for St. Bernard's parish in Levittown, New York and facilitates support groups, trains caregivers of the newly bereaved, and gives workshops at the annual Diocesan bereavement conference.

Sabatini has written two books on bereavement: *Bereavement Counseling in the School Setting* and *Lessons Learned on Grief*, and a memoir: *Luciano: an Immigrant's Journey of Rediscovery*. His education includes BA and MS degrees from Hunter College, a PD from Hofstra University, and a PhD from Columbia Pacific University.

He lives in Blue Point, New York with his wife Suzanne.

For further information, visit his bereavement website at www.empoweringthebereaved.com and author website www.lucianosabatini.com.

# OTHER BOOKS BY LUCIANO SABATINI

We are a death phobic society. Consequently, we provide very little help to our citizens in dealing with the one common denominator that we all face, the death of those we love.

The paucity of death education programs in our elementary and secondary schools is evident of our death avoidance culture. Although many of our schools do attempt to assist the thousands of children and adolescents yearly who lose parents, siblings, and other loved ones, their efforts tend to focus on how to assist the newly bereaved student in the days immediately following the loss. Very few schools have a long term approach that extends far beyond the immediate crisis, seeking to assist students with the life altering changes that follow the death of a family member.